Copyr

yhen.baki@gmail.com
https://www.jbaki.com/

Special thanks to Jarret Middleton (Darkansas), my developmental editor, Mary Anne Balch Speigel, my wife, life mate, and fellow writer, my daughters, Jessica and Liz, and all my friends, teachers, and colleagues at Hugo House in Seattle WA for their patience and support while I fretted over Braided.

ISBN Paperback: 978-0-937977-08-8
Ebook: 978-0-937977-09-5

Library of Congress Control Number 2021904689

Overwhelmed by the discovery of her mother's deception and the secrets of her ancestor's origins, a young Seattleite slips deeper into prescription opioid addiction. Braided tells the story of how she discovers her true purpose during a deadly fentanyl overdose.

Mira's body lies lifeless in her designer recliner, an empty pill bottle on the floor beside her. Her frozen eyes are no longer able to see the Seattle city lights sparkling below, and her lungs no longer able to breathe the fresh Puget Sound air. Joined by the spirit of Jakob, who departed his body lying dead on the bloody battlefield of Lexington, Massachusetts on April 19, 1775, their spirits hover together near the ceiling of her downtown high-rise.

Braided is an eloquently woven story about a modern woman whose evolving view of herself and the world captures the readers attention from the first word to the last. Mr. Speigel creates compelling characters with unique voices and perspectives. The psychological twists and turns will have the reader embracing the not not true nature of her humanity.

CHRISTINA CAHILL, DIRECTOR, HUMANITAS

My first impression was....Wow, what a terrific beach read! I'm enjoying the sun and salty breeze as I read a hugely entertaining and accessible book. Then you had me. The story turned deeper and deeper, more complex and shaded. Ultimately Braided is a story and study of human foibles, family systems and dysfunction, religious thought, Holocaust, theology, and mysticism.

RABBI SAMUEL K. JOSEPH, PHD

PROFESSOR EMERITUS, HEBREW UNION COLLEGE

For My Daughters,
Jessica and Elizabeth,
who helped teach me what is not not true.

BRAIDED

A Not Not True Story

Robert Speigel

Speigel and Associates Inc

PROLOGUE

The lead projectile pierced his eyebrow, spun him around, and brought the two of them face to face. His eyes stretched wide and lifeless, as blood spilled from the gaping hole just under his hairline. The fluid braided into crimson rivulets that weaved down both sides of his nose, over his chin, then disappeared into the brick-red fabric of his colonial military coat. While his comrade collapsed onto the lush grass of the Lexington Town Green, Jakob broke into a full sprint, disappearing into the trees before his friend's face hit the ground.

Moments earlier, they'd marched together into the field of battle to the rhythm and tones of the drum and fife corps. Jakob's position had been second from the left in the third line of infantry, just a few steps from the tree line. The lieutenant told them the enemy would advance into range and engage them as they stood waiting, perhaps 125 to 150 yards away. They were not to shoot until the enemy fired their first volley. The lieutenant demanded the front line drop to one knee and raise their muskets into the ready position as the line behind raised their muskets in unison. Both lines of colonials would fire a fusillade after the enemy fired. Heavy casualties always accompanied this timeworn and formal method of warfare.

Jakob had been scanning the horizon for a sign of the enemy's presence when his comrade had spun and faced him. He'd heard no shot ring out; only the sound of the fife and drum prevailed. A force unknown to him over which he had no control demanded he retreat and run for his life. His military training had not prepared him for this. Only a few years earlier, he'd been playing with friends on hot summer days. They would swing from a rope they'd hung in the branches overhanging the lake to drop into the cool water below. Nothing could have prepared him for this.

The sound of branches snapping underfoot signaled he was not alone.

Danke Gott, Jakob thought to himself in his native Hessian tongue. Perhaps others had run with him.

"Find the coward; don't let him get away!" an officer shouted.

Jakob dropped his musket to the ground, wriggled out of his rucksack, and fled. The sound of boots pounding ground only a few yards behind filled his ears. Knowing he could not outrun them, Jakob dove into a heavy thicket of winterberry bushes and sank to the ground, disappearing—or so he thought.

Silence surrounded him. He buried his face in his sleeve to quiet his quick and shallow breath. Sweat ran over his scalp, down his forehead, and off the end of his nose. He lay motionless in the bushes, his mind filled with the image of crimson blood flowing down his friend's face. He'd seen other faces contorted with shock and pain as their bodies fell, first to their knees, then face down into the sweet grass below. The dense weave of foliage surrounding him refused to muffle the continuing cacophony of musket blasts —lead balls finding home, unforgiving. The stench of gunpowder and death filled his nostrils. He burrowed deeper into the tangle of winterberry.

Without warning, vise-like hands seized Jakob's ankles and dragged him from his lair. He looked away from his comrades' faces.

"Coward, deserter, you sorry excuse for a man," they shouted at him. "You're worthless and a failure. You are nothing."

Without warning, searing pain pierced Jakob's chest. A spike of war impaled him, exiting through his back—the bayonet of his own superior officer. Exquisite agony burned a path through his shoulder blade. Jakob turned away from his executioner, unable to look into his eyes.

Mortal shame dripped from his being. Black shrouds of worthlessness transformed him into a paltry being of no value. He reeked of inferiority, destined to die a failure. The officer's thrust dispatched Jakob to hell, forever immersing him in shame and dishonor. He believed no one would remember him; they would forget him for all time. As his lifeblood spilled into the soil beneath him and his breathing slowed to nothingness, a single question passed through his dying mind: Was this my only purpose in life?

His eyes opened for one last look of life. His executioner stood over him, gripping his stiletto spear in place as his rage-filled eyes spilled over with disgust. Jakob stared into the brick-red of his lieutenant's field jacket. His disgust became Jakob's disgust. Jakob branded himself a coward and a traitor with no human worth, destined to travel for eternity without redemption.

As Jakob's eyes shuddered and closed for the last time, his gaze fell upon the officer's right shoulder, bringing into focus a single silken aiguillette adorning the sleeve of his field coat. The braided scarlet rope filled his eyes as he sank into darkness.

Cold swaddled him.

Oblivion enveloped him.

A final shallow breath entered Jakob's lungs, only to remain unbreathed.

All was still . . . all was still.

All but for the sound of a distant, imperceptible voice.

| 1 |

The two women talking at the table behind the window at the Starbucks distracted Mira from her mission as she walked by. Both ladies sported graying ginger hair, one with it double braided to each side of her head and the other with a long single thick braid hanging down from the center. They wore dresses of a forgotten era, flowered, old European.

The two paused their conversation and looked at her in unison. Did they know her? Their expressions invited her to join them—to take a break from her hurried chaos, to have a cup of tea, and sit and talk with them for just a moment.

Mira's face flushed red, and panic rushed through her body. She turned her head to the street, where she imagined everyone in the passing cars was looking directly at her. Her heart pounded in her chest, and her breathing stopped. She turned back to the table a second later but found it empty. Her eyes dropped to the sidewalk as she reached out to the wall of the building to steady herself.

She hated these moments when reality merged with unreality. They were nightmarish and frightened her and becoming more frequent in the last few months. Becoming used to them scared her the most. She leaned up against the building for a moment to catch her breath. A passerby stopped to ask her if she was alright. She answered she was fine. Perhaps the stress of work was getting to her, and she hadn't been sleeping well. Finally, she pulled herself together, refocused on her goal, and brought her eyes forward. The doorway to the Walgreens was just a few steps away, and she soon found herself in line at the pharmacy counter after stopping to pick up her needed props.

As she stood waiting for her turn at the counter, Mira felt beads of sweat break from her armpits. She cycled between Instagram and Twitter on her iPhone while moving up to the next position in line. The moistness in her palms and the subtle twitch of her right hand betrayed her calm facade.

Why is that bitch taking so long to check out? she thought. What could they be talking about?

Off to her left, a clean-cut guy at the cold and flu shelf caught her attention, interrupting her mind rant. Was he a store dick? Mira had scanned the aisles looking for any plainclothes security people on her way to the prescription department, but she hadn't noticed him until now. Her heartbeat quickened, and a metallic taste entered her mouth. A quick right turn would get her the fuck out of there, but she'd taken her last oxy this morning, and she needed more now.

The red and black Sudafed boxes lined up on the shelf next to the suspicious guy caught her attention. Mira's heart raced, and her vision fuzzed. She felt lightheaded, and her knees weakened. "Fuck . . . Fuck!" She muttered to herself. "Pull it together," but the delusion had already taken over. The red background printed on the sides of the Sudafed boxes started to bleed out and weave into the ginger braids of the women she'd seen sitting back at the Starbucks. Finally, her vision completely washed over in red and transported her out of the Walgreens.

Now, she walked on her way home from middle school on a brisk November day. She stopped for a bag of chips and a soft drink at her neighborhood drugstore. As she walked to the checkout counter, she looked around to make sure no one watched and placed herself behind a column away from the store video camera. Then, she reached out to scoop a box of Sudafed off the shelf and drop it unnoticed into her schoolbag.

She'd started abusing Sudafed in seventh grade after a pediatrician prescribed it for an acute sinus infection. Besides relieving her congestion, she'd discovered it provided the kick she needed to wake up at 7:00 a.m. every day to get to school and stay awake. So she took it almost every day, honing her technique for shoplifting it from drugstores around town. Her mother never knew, or at least never noticed.

"Fuck," said Mira, reaching out into space next to her, seeking any solid object available to steady herself as her mind returned to the present.

"Are you OK?" asked a woman behind her.

"I'm OK," Mira mumbled back.

Mira looked up to see that the pharmacy counter had cleared, so she refocused her attention on the task at hand. She stepped forward and slowed her breathing to regain her composure. She looked at the floor and formed the hint of a seductive smile at the corner of her mouth as she walked. At the counter, Mira placed her carefully selected props onto the counter beside the cash register and looked up at the pharmacist. She fumbled through her purse before pulling a crisp slip of paper out, along with her health insurance card.

Hidden beneath her blood-red silken blouse and slate-grey corporate suit jacket, a sleeve of colorful tattoos crept from her wrist to her shoulder. Spikes of hair dyed black to cover her naturally curly ginger locks and trimmed short framed her forehead and ears. She concealed her waxed ginger eyebrows with a similar camouflage of onyx dye. A single slender crimson braid crept down her nape and disappeared behind the fabric of her jacket. Soft curves of subtle cleavage peeked out from the carefully positioned lapels of her blouse, framing her diminutive chest. And yet, her precisely constructed persona encrusted a fragile and deeply fissured spirit.

She raised her head, locked eyes with the man wearing the starched-white smock, and held out the slip. His eyes, fiftyish and tired, darted to the deep-blue box of Trojan Extra Ribbed condoms she'd deposited on the counter. She noticed his breath quicken a little. Was she too obvious?

The pharmacist looked up at her for a moment before his eyes fell back to the prescription slip he held between his thumb and forefinger. It was a perfect replica of the real thing, right down to the logo she'd lifted from the Polyclinic website and the unreadable signature of the imaginary doctor who'd penned it. It had taken her all of fifteen minutes to mock it up in Adobe Illustrator. While he read it, her gaze darted back and scanned for the guy at the cold-and-flu counter. Where was he? She located him over by first aid. Did he see her looking? She could still walk away, but the pharmacist already held the evidence of her crime in his hand with her name all over it. His eyes moved back to hers once more. When their eyes met again, she tilted her head a bit to the right and reminded herself to breathe.

The pharmacist snuck a glance at her subtle exposure, then went back to the condoms before picking up the prescription slip. She wondered for an instant if he believed the slip was legit, then noticed he rerouted his attention back to the curve of her cleavage and the package of Trojan condoms.

He cleared his throat. "Give me a few minutes; I'll have this right up for you."

While she waited at the counter, a small voice inside her wondered if she had tried this once too often. She imagined Seattle police officers emerging from behind the counter, cuff.ing her, throwing her in the back seat of a cruiser, and carting her off to fake-prescription jail. She escaped that thought by fuming about the previous eight hours she'd spent at Amazon dealing with her boss.

Growing at an insane pace, Amazon had little

regard for humanistic screening or training for their personnel. As a result, their ill-prepared and inexperienced employees struggled to perform complex tasks when promoted.

Amazon had recruited Mira eight months earlier. They'd stolen her away from her position at Microsoft, her first job after completing her undergraduate training. She'd worked at Microsoft for eight years as a project manager, made good money, and had her stock options vested. But boredom plagued her, and she needed a change. Her friends played musical chairs with the voracious Seattle tech companies and convinced her to join them after Amazon gobbled them up.

Alcohol, weed, and parties had been her primary majors in college. She'd completed her bachelor of arts in business, thinking everyone needed to know about business, didn't they? Unfortunately, she'd created no clear visions of her personal or professional goals, and now she made way too much money as a "Bus Dev" manager at Amazon to alter her course. Some part of her knew that she'd traded one rut for another when she left Microsoft. Hell, she hardly knew what business development meant and wondered if her boss knew. Everyone at Amazon seemed more concerned about maintaining "headcount" than job performance.

During her sophomore year of college, she took Introduction to Psychology to round out her schedule and became intrigued by much of the content. Although she couldn't explain it, some. Thing in it resonated with her in a way she'd never experienced before. Then, one day during class, she read a quote from Carl Jung and burst into tears. He said, "One does not become enlightened by imagining figures of light, but by making the darkness conscious."

As she read his words, tears filled her eyes. Then, through a thick veil of grief, a dark and terrifying image emerged for an instant: a python directly in front of her face with eyes glowing orange-red. The viper disappeared as quickly as it had come. A teaching assistant noticed and approached her after class, asking if she was all right. She said she was fine, turned around, and walked out of class. She disappeared before the assistant had time to tell her about the free counseling center available to her on campus.

Mira was the only home-grown Seattleite in her multicultural division at Amazon. Her natural scholastic aptitude, paired with her second-place academic standing in her high school graduating class and her multiethnic look, earned her a full-ride scholarship through Stanford's School of Business. After she earned her undergraduate degree, they enticed her to remain in California to complete her MBA, with the offer of an assistantship that included living expenses. Microsoft recruiters were all over the Stanford campus, and she returned to Seattle with a lucrative job offer in hand. But, by then, the ghosts lurking in the hazy fog of her maturing addiction had taken up permanent residence.

"Can I ring up your other items now as well?"

The pharmacist startled Mira back into the present. He'd returned, holding a small prescription bag stapled and pregnant with cargo.

"Just the prescription for now," Mira replied. "I need to pick up some toothpaste on the way out." While the pharmacist ran her credit card, she fished her cell phone out of her bag, clicked on the Uber app, and ordered a black car. Her nerves were shrieking for attention. She walked to the front of the store and returned the Trojans to where she'd found them. She slipped out the door of the Walgreens with sixty, 80-milligram time-released oxys in her bag. Able to breathe again, Mira felt ecstatic. She'd done it! She walked around the corner, ripped open the bag, popped the cap from the bottle of small-white orbs, and crunched one between her teeth. Her screaming nerves quieted as she waited on the curb for her Uber to arrive.

| 2 |

Her car arrived outside the pharmacy precisely
two minutes after her request. She slipped into the
back seat of the spacious BMW and popped one more
of her treasures into her mouth, immediately crush-
ing it to dust. The rush of euphoria transformed into
warm bliss as the opium seeped into her tongue and
invaded her blood. Her body sank further into the soft
leather seat as she descended deeper into the dreamy
fog of the oxys. She flowed from a state of ecstatic
floating to one of a juicy turn-on. By the time the
driver reached the entrance of her building, the stress
of the crazy day at Amazon had dissolved into history. As the car pulled to a gentle stop outside her
building, she slid across the smooth black leather seat
and floated out through the spacious door onto the
waiting curb. Her boyfriend Ian should be home by
now. She imagined he would slip his hands down the
back of her slacks to stroke her bare bottom when he
greeted her at the door.

Mira lived on the twenty-third floor of the Insignia Towers, just to the south of the Westlake Mall
in downtown Seattle. Unlike the sprawling suburban
malls of the Midwest states, West-lake Mall comprised

four stories of Tiffany-like jewelry stores, gift shops, and exclusive clothiers. The top-floor food court offered a wide variety of ethnic foods to the thousands of workers in the surrounding high-rise office buildings. They'd extended the old 1963 World's Fair Monorail to make nonstop runs every thirty minutes between Seattle Center and Westlake Mall, ending at a third-floor station.

They'd completed the forty-one-story, glass-encrusted Insignia Towers just seven months earlier. Seattle held the lead in the country for the total number of towering building cranes lurking over the downtown landscape. Like the stoic great blue heron Mira spotted as she jogged the bike trail along Lake Washington Boulevard to Seward Park, the construction cranes methodically turned their heads on slender steel necks, lifting heavy loads of steel and concrete as they stacked floor upon floor of the rising Seattle skyline. Bright navy blue and brilliant-green neon lights adorned the building cranes in honor of the Seattle Seahawks football team. They created eerie streaks that sliced through the darkened Seattle sky at night. The sweeping view from Mira's twenty-third-floor, one-bedroom condo overlooked Pike Place Market and the Seattle waterfront below, then continued out over Elliott Bay across to Bainbridge Island.

On clear days, the distant Olympic Mountains peeked above the low morning fog that hugged the chilly waters of the bay before coming into magnificent fullness as the sun warmed the heavy mist into oblivion. Mira sat for hours, looking out over that view. Evenings when she came home from work, she munched a few THC gummies and imagined sailing out of that bay on a beautiful sailboat. She dreamed of traveling with the man of her dreams—handsome and strong, quiet and attentive, intelligent and loving, loyal and committed, up through the Straits of Juan de Fuca, out into the Great Pacific Ocean, all the way to the Far East to explore hidden coves and mysterious lands. Some days she imagined it might even happen. It never crossed her mind she could do it on her own.

The stark reality of Mira's life always brought her crashing back to reality. She struggled with the burdens of everyday stressors. She'd taken an interest-only, full-price, no-down-payment mortgage to qualify for the one-and-a-quarter million-dollar price tag of her brand-new condo. All the nouveau riche of Seattle's recently transplanted high-tech millennials were doing it. One thousand new overpaid and financially naïve residents moved into Seattle every week. Reasonably priced housing no longer existed. They called it San Francisco North.

Mira didn't understand the financial implications of her impulsive decision. Her inflated ego believed she knew what she was doing . . . the mortgage broker deftly explained it all to her in reassuring terms: With her $10,500 per month net paycheck, she could easily afford the $3,475 mortgage payment and still have enough left over to fund her 40K and health savings accounts. The housing market was inflating over 10 percent per year, so she'd make money from the increase in value, while her bloated Amazon salary would only multiply each year. It seemed like a perfect plan, save for the nagging queasiness in her stomach every time she paid her mortgage payment.

Mira's father would've told her that her return on investment would be "on the come;" that her interest-only mortgage payment represented rent from the mortgage company, who hoped the place would inflate in value. He would've warned her that if the economy went into a downturn or Amazon itself suffered from corporate dysfunction, she could lose everything.

Mira never really knew her father since he left her so long ago and wondered if he was sophisticated enough to know such things. She wanted to believe he was and wanted to believe she could make an intelligent decision. The condo location offered her a short trolley ride to and from her office on South Lake Union, and the place had a view that wowed her friends. Mira had a reputation for making impulsive decisions, and buying her condo was no exception. She had so much oxy in her the day she signed the papers, she'd almost nodded off.

Anxiety and loneliness plagued Mira. She kept it well hidden, but inside, a small voice reminded her she was missing a vital element that everyone else possessed: it told her she possessed a fatal flaw. She felt disconnected and alone in the world. Most times, her palms were moist and clammy, and she picked at her cuticles until they bled.

Alcohol and drugs became her welcome companion. In grade school, along with the discovery of Sudafed, she'd started snitching drinks from her mother's open bottles of red wine left re-corked on the dining-room sideboard and from the whiskey jugs she discovered in a cabinet under the kitchen sink. Later, in high school, she discovered how to use cocaine to energize her days, followed by oxys to calm her nights. She bought cocaine on the street with money she made babysitting or hooked from her mother's purse. It was easy for her and her friends to raid their family's medicine cabinets for pharmaceutical uppers and pain meds. As an adult, she adeptly manipulated doctors, prescriptions, and pharmacies to keep her supply of oxys intact. The sixty she just scored would last her a good two weeks.

When her Uber pulled up outside her building, Mira exited and crossed over the sidewalk to the front door. The smart key-card buried in her purse automatically activated the lock, and she heard it click as it disengaged. A computer voice declared, "Welcome home, Ms. Shaw." She glided through the security door into the lobby, slid onto the waiting elevator as it beeped a robotic-sounding signal recognizing her ID, and heard the computer voice report, "Floor 23, Ms. Shaw, Accepted."

She wanted to stay high for Ian's greeting as she felt the opioid in her blood metabolizing away. She reached into her purse to retrieve one more of her small snow-white friends and quickly crunched it down. The warm bliss streamed through her body as she slipped through the front door.

Ian's musky scent greeted her first as the oxy

heightened her senses. His pheromones triggered a sexy warmth that trickled down from her navel. She located him—predictably shirtless—in the kitchen chopping carrots and onions on the island. Hardly a square inch of bare skin showed through the intricate collage of tattoos covering his slender frame. A nameless nude image on his left forearm sported plump breasts bulging out below a crown of twelve pentacles that encircled her forehead. Her face reflected Mother Mary's features. The image did not exactly offend Mira, but she imagined Ian preferred the ample chest displayed on his arm to her own diminutive form. At first, the image repulsed her, but, over time, she'd learned to make it invisible.

Standing at the door of her kitchen, the scent of his skin invaded her nose, and his essence invaded her cells. The chemical reaction transported Mira back to her first encounter with Ian at the Underground in Sodo. She'd walked in with her friend Amanda, paid her cover, looked up, and saw him onstage. He looked nerdy and short, but Mira couldn't resist the intense vibration that seared through her as he played his piercing guitar riffs. Ian's fingers flew over the neck of his Fender Stratocaster guitar, channeling the spirit of Stevie Ray Vaughan and Jimi Hendrix. He hadn't reached their level of ease and confidence with his instrument, but Mira couldn't tell the difference. She stopped for a moment, closed her eyes, and listened to Ian's gravelly voice wailing Stevie Ray's bluesy lyrics. A sexy warmth rose in her. Mira imagined he was singing directly to her.

Well, I love my baby . . . like the finest wine.
Stick with her until the end of time.
She's my sweet little thang . . . she's my pride and joy.
She's my sweet little baby . . . I'm her little lover boy.

She took him home that night and started molesting him in the back seat of the Uber before the driver pulled away from the curb. Alcohol and oxys coursed through her veins, and the compulsion to have sex with men as quickly as possible overruled her better judgment. She wasn't horny—quite the opposite. She felt nervous as hell. Her mind raced: Does he like me? If I don't come on to him, will he think I'm uptight?

She knew how to silence her chaotic thoughts. As soon as they hit the back seat, she flipped herself over his lap and straddled his waist, facing him. His sizeable bulge grew under her as she ground her pelvis into his and buried her tongue deep into his mouth. The taste of his cigarettes and alcohol offended her, but she liked the power she felt rising in his jeans and her own moistness penetrating her pants. She knew exactly how to slide herself on top of men to drive them crazy. Their clothes started coming off in the elevator on the way up to her condo, startling the couple who joined them on the fourth floor on their way up to the roof garden.

The next morning, as Mira slowly roused from her comatose slumber, the words of Stevie Ray Vaughan echoed in her memory:

I need some kind of kindness . . .
Some kind of sympathy; oh, no.
We're stranded . . .
Caught in the crossfire.

The empty pillow next to her when she rolled over the next morning didn't surprise her. She expected one-night stands and found them preferable to uncomfortable mutual wake-ups. The remnants of narcotics, alcohol, and sex in her system made room for a nagging headache and nausea when she remembered she had a brunch planned with girlfriends. She wandered into the bathroom, sat down on the toilet to pee, and stuck her nose into her armpit to determine if a shower was in order.

She let out a yelp when Ian, carrying a hot mug of strong black coffee and a slice of multigrain toast topped with butter and raspberry jam, walked right in and caught her sniffing. She hoped the flush on her face went unnoticed.

Ian sat down on the floor in front of the toilet, munching his toast, and said, "What are your plans today?"

Talking with a man while sitting on the toilet made Mira blush. She tried her best to appear unfazed. "I need to jump in the shower and then meet some friends for brunch at Lowell's in the market. We'll probably head over to Pacific Place afterward to do some girl shopping and hang out. You're welcome to take a shower and relax here. If you like," Mira added quietly, hoping he'd leave.

"Yeah, I'll probably take a quick shower and get

out of here."

After Mira finished dressing, she found Ian sitting on the couch in her living room, drinking coffee and watching MSNBC. She breathed a sigh of relief that he wasn't a Fox News fan. She left her visitor keycard for him on the coffee table in case he needed to get back in for anything, gave him a hesitant and uncomfortable kiss on the lips, and quickly slipped out the front door.

When Mira returned home that evening, the previous night's events formed a distant and hazy memory. She'd stayed clean and sober all day to prepare for returning to work the next morning. Drinking or using on work nights or during work days was a bad idea, although living in a marijuana-legal state allowed for intermittent midweek partying. In her mind, the encounter with the musician was just that: an encounter.

When she glanced into her living room after securing the front door, she noticed three guitars perched on stands in the corner. Two amps and various electronic equipment sat close by. Her distant memory suddenly snapped into sharp focus. In the guest bedroom, she found men's clothes hanging in the walk-in closet and men's toiletries scattered on the bathroom countertop. She felt heat rising from her neck and flushing her face, but not the heat of desire.

"What the fuck is going on here?" she said to no one in particular.

Wonderful aromas wafted from the kitchen and filled the condo with a homey fragrance, interrupting her anger. Mira followed the sweet smells and peeked her head into the kitchen.

Ian stood shirtless at the kitchen island, giving her the chance to scan his bare upper body under the bright can-lights recessed into her kitchen ceiling. In the dark shadows the night before, and during the heat of their sex, she hadn't noticed how tatted out his torso was. She looked for any trace of unadorned skin. She thought the sleeve of tatts covering her left arm was impressive, but Ian's array was amazing.

He skillfully deboned a full side of watermelon-pink Alaskan king salmon and sliced it into healthy two-inch-wide strips as he hummed to himself not noticing her standing at the doorway. She watched as he carefully transferred each piece of the Pacific delicacy into a parchment-paper-lined roasting pan. He deftly brushed them with a healthy layer of rich-brown Dijon mustard, then drizzled on ribbons of Oregon sage honey, finishing the coating with a dusting of finely diced walnuts. A second roasting pan filled with assorted sliced green and yellow zucchini, Brussel sprouts, Walla Walla sweet onions, and pencil-thin asparagus doused with extra-virgin olive oil and Tamari sauce sat poised on top of the stove, ready for the oven. Mira's interior decorator had fully outfitted the kitchen for many types of cooking, but this was the very first time anyone had used it.

Ian often crashed with friends or acquaintances for weeks or months at a time. Gigging didn't provide the stable income that allowed for a leased place to live. His rock star ego took Mira's hot seduction the previous night as an invitation to hang out for a while.

"Hi," Mira announced, not knowing what else to say.

Startled, Ian turned his head to the doorway and blurted, "Oh. Hi. How are you doin? Want a glass of wine?"

His casual demeanor disarmed Mira, and she forgot what she'd intended to say to him about moving his stuff into her house. Before she knew what was happening, over two years had passed.

| 3 |

On a brisk fall day during their first year together, Ian and Mira sat over brunch on the deck of the Eastlake Bar and Grill overlooking Lake Union, and the cut headed into the Ballard Locks. Ian sipped his second Bloody Mary and looked like shit. One more Saturday morning, one more hangover.

Ian rarely talked about himself, but on this morning, as they munched on English muffins and ham and cheese omelets, he opened about his childhood. He shared how he grew up in Bellingham, about ninety miles north of Seattle. He told her about attending high school and one year of college there, studying psychology before dropping out. When he was eleven, he'd picked up a used Squier guitar and a 15-watt amp at a garage sale and never put it down. In those early days, he was into the heavy metal bands of the day, like Metallica and Def Leppard, that dominated the mainstream music scene in the late 1980s.

"I traded my practice amp for a stage amp and set up a practice area in the garage," he said.

He put down his fork for a moment and, with his eyes on his plate, said, "I kept the volume up high enough to drown out the drunken brawls between mom and dad, especially when my aunts and uncles came around. The neighbors called the police to complain about my loud music but never mentioned the screaming coming from the people in the house. I'm sure the police must have noticed my mother's bruised face and arms when she answered the door. They came back to the garage and had me turn down the volume, but they never asked me about the violence in my family. My father finally moved out when I was fifteen, under a restraining order brought by the court's domestic-violence program that allowed me and mom to stay in the house after they divorced."

Ian told Mira that, after his father left, he became addicted to the music of Jimi Hendrix. He couldn't believe Jimi was self-taught.

"Hendrix somehow taught himself to play on a right-handed guitar that he played left-handed after he'd restrung it with the strings flipped over. But, when his father was around, Jimi would flip the guitar over and play it right-handed as his father demanded, even though everything was reversed," Ian explained, as Mira's eyes glazed over trying to comprehend what he was saying.

He told her how he studied the work of Hendrix and Stevie Rae Vaughan. How Vaughan had played the guitar at seven years of age, rose to fame in the mid-1980s, and died in a helicopter crash in 1990 when he was only thirty-five. His audiences knew him as SRV, and he was one of the best guitarists in rock and blues history.

Ian shared how he'd formed a ragtag pickup

group in Bellingham and started gigging in the local college taverns and clubs. He shared how he'd worked on graveling his voice by chain smoking Winston cigarettes and weed, and built on the singing experience he'd developed screaming Metallica in the garage as a kid. He scraped by financially until he moved down to Seattle to find a talent manager who booked regular gigs for him.

Mira learned a lot about Ian's life that day, but his stories lacked any feelings he had about his experiences. Their conversation over brunch left her with a familiar feeling of incompleteness—detachment. On one level, she admired his simplicity and longed to have a mind that ran at his speed. But she also longed to feel connected to him emotionally. Were they "boyfriend/ girlfriend?" she asked herself. "Was he the 'one'?"

While she had dated lots of men, she would name none of them as her "boyfriend." The concepts of "being in love" or "getting married" made her hyperventilate. Deep bouts of loneliness and depression followed her life of one-night stands and fantasies of being swept off her feet. Her brunch with Ian left her more confused about her relationship with him than ever. Were they moving forward or idling in neutral?

| 4 |

One warm summer day, when Mira and her teenage friends were hanging out at the Evergreen State Fair in Monroe, Amanda started screwing around with a corn dog she'd bought. Amanda was the group jokester and enjoyed acting sexually provocative. She took her corn dog, started licking it along its entire length, and kissed the tip. Then she sucked it, moving it in and out of her mouth while moaning and moving her hips. Suddenly, she pushed the entire length of it all the way down her throat, making gagging sounds and moaning as if she were coming. While the rest of her friends cracked up in raucous laughter, Mira freaked out in a full-blown panic attack.

Unable to breathe, a pair of orange-red serpent eyes peered into Mira's eyes. She was four years old again, back in that musky basement playroom of the daycare house, where her mother left her every day, the adults lounging upstairs, disinterested and disengaged. The older kids bullied her and scared her there. She had first seen those orange-red eyes lurking in the dark corners of that basement and then later elsewhere.

When her friends saw Mira's reaction, they sat her down and talked her down until she could breathe again. Mira knew about blow jobs from porn movies she'd watched with friends, so why the panic attack when Amanda started screwing around with a corn dog? She hid her panic from her friends and told no one about her vision. She figured it was normal. She knew she'd have to learn to give blow jobs to have boyfriends, so she learned to do it well and get them over with. She also carried lingering resentment.

But Ian had an insatiable thirst for sex regularly. Most days, he woke up with a raging hard-on that he presented to Mira like a trophy he'd just won at a tournament. "You gotta see this," he'd announce. "Feel it." He pulled her hand over to grab it like a baseball bat, then waited patiently, wanting more. She sleepily obliged with gentle rubs and tugs, knowing what he expected next.

Bedtime at night with Ian brought a different expectation. He'd climb into bed, swing one leg over Mira's waist, and kiss her deeply, probing her tongue with his. If Mira yawned and tried to turn away, Ian seemed not to notice or care. If she tried to dissuade him, he whimpered like a desolate puppy begging for table scraps. Most times, she quietly accommodated him, believing it was her duty to do so. An adept lover, he made sure he lasted until she came, her orgasm triggering his. When exhaustion overwhelmed her, and she had no interest in coming, her practiced fake orgasm finished him quickly. Then he'd roll off, clean himself with a small towel, and offer it to Mira for her clean up. He never offered the towel to her first. He'd roll over, facing away from her and fall into a deep sleep. The next day usually duplicated the last.

Their habits around alcohol and drugs were similar, but different as well. Before Ian moved in, Mira enjoyed cocktails before dinner out with friends or at a club before concerts. She occasionally substituted THC for nicotine juice on a vape break during work. She kept her stashes of coke and oxys for special occasions, and, although they were becoming a staple of her day, she still considered those to be "party" drugs. Her lexicon didn't include the words addiction or addict.

But Ian was something else. He bought beer by the case at Costco and stopped regularly at one of the three Uncle Ike's Pot Shops to pick up his weekly stash of ganja and edibles meant for daily consumption. After his friends left, Mira found the residue of coke lines on the coffee table. When Ian wasn't looking, she mopped up the leftovers with her index finger, depositing the white treasure onto her eager gums.

Mira wondered what Ian might be like sober. She could not keep up with his drug and alcohol use and still function at work or socially. Over time, when his friends were over and lines of coke appeared, they asked her to join in for a line or two. She found the drug intriguing and liked the energy it provided. After using, she learned to take Benadryl to bring her down enough to get to sleep, and, sometimes, she drank wine or whiskey before bed when the Benadryl didn't work fast enough.

Over time, Mira wondered if she loved Ian, if "he was the one." She wondered if she'd reached the age when settling down with one guy was the next prescribed step. She had doubts about Ian, but then she had doubts about every man she'd ever thought about as a partner. One of her friends once said, "Imagine having children with him. If you want to have children with him, he's probably the one."

But what if the thought of having children at all freaked you out to the max? Mira couldn't imagine herself as a mother, much less a wife, and the subject usually brought out the oxy bot.tle. Plus, Ian was a fucking rocker! She was a thirty-something living with a rocker who moved into her house after a night of debauchery and never left. Is that the foundation for a long-term relationship?

But after the last two years with Ian, Mira's life had settled into a stable, predictable, secure routine. If she'd been seeing a therapist, her diagnosis might have been clinical depression, but it never crossed her mind that something was wrong. Why would she need a therapist? All her friends were jealous of her. Living in downtown Seattle with a sexy musician boyfriend, making close to a double six-figure income, traveling when she wanted, building her 401k, paying off her student loans; what could be better? So why was she bored, unhappy, and writing fake prescriptions every few weeks to keep up with her growing opioid needs?

| 5 |

Thinking it might keep the pharmacists from sniffing out her game, or that she might run out of pharmacies to scam, Mira started sprinkling in a few scripts for fentanyl on her trips to different pharmacies around the city and suburbs. Her appetite had increased, so not to need so much, she tried to spread out her use. That started stringing her out and making her irritable. She'd read online about a plant product called kratom that mimicked the effects of opioids, and she started using that during the day. It definitely helped, but nothing could take the place of oxycodone and fentanyl. She was trying her best to avoid the panic growing in her gut.

Mira's days at Amazon were routine and boring. She'd settled into a decent team with a boss who could actually teach her something about business development. Her new department developed creative ways to deliver interactive content to children as an alternative to the mind-numbing video games parents used to mollify them while busy with their own interests. She grew up as a daycare kid with a full-time working mother and an absent father, so her history provided a perfect backdrop for her new job. Providing content to help children pass endless hours without human contact held positive meaning for Mira.

She liked to walk to work a little early, pick up a double-tall latte at the Uptown Coffee Shop, and stop at the "Spheres" Amazon built in the middle of Seattle. The Spheres comprised three massive glass geodesic structures that created a terrarium-like environment for over 40,000 plants and trees from the cloud forest regions of over thirty countries. Visitors spent hours getting high on the health benefits of the negative ions created by the immense trees and plants. Amazon meant the Spheres as a sanctuary for its employees to rest, relax, meditate, and create. It also enjoyed the community brownie points the structures earned, even though its image as an uncaring corporate giant driving up the cost of living and income disparity in Seattle into the stratosphere remained unabated.

On this day, Mira emerged from the front door of the main Sphere and noticed an older African American man perched on a bench right outside the door. Most of the time, she forgot about her own bronze complexion, shying away from contact with other people of color. But today, an unknown force pulled her to sit with the African-skinned man on the bench. He looked about seventy years old, with tightly woven salt-and-pepper hair. He wore aging Levi's, a vintage, plaid-flannel shirt, and a navy-blue baseball cap with battle ribbons and the words "Vietnam Veteran" emblazoned across the front. His eyes were dark brown and crystal clear, without a single streak of bloodshot. Without pausing, Mira settled down next to him.

He looked straight ahead at the people coming in and out of the Sphere.

"My dad died in Iraq," she mumbled without thinking. "I don't remember him much. He was African American."

"I wondered where you got that beautiful skin of yours," said the Vet.

She hadn't seen him notice.

"Thank you for your service," the old man continued, still looking straight ahead. "Your father's sacrifice makes you a Gold Star Family Member. It's like you served with him. It's how we honor and recognize the sacrifice the family makes when it loses a member in service of our country."

A waterfall of tears fell down Mira's face, but she was still on autopilot. The two of them looked straight ahead.

"I'm so sad about what's happened to our wonderful city," the veteran continued. "I was born here in 1949, out on the Peninsula. My dad logged for Weyerhaeuser out there. He wanted something better for his kids, so he moved us over to Seattle and bought us a broken-down old house in the Central District for just over $11,000. He logged during the week, coming home on the weekends, and worked on the house. Dad made enough so Mom didn't have to work, so she stayed home and cared for us kids. When I graduated from high school, Vietnam got most of us Black kids from the inner city. Hell, what did we know? We didn't know nuthin about what that war was about. There was the draft, and we weren't goin to college, so we went off to do our service. I did two tours before I got shot up. It was so bloody—I don't even remember most of it. Probably better that way. . . how did your dad die? Is he buried at Arlington?"

The suddenness and directness of the question shocked Mira. No one ever asked her how her dad died. No one had told her the details. No one ever acknowledged he was dead. Hell, no one ever asked if she had a dad. She'd never visited his grave and didn't know where they buried him.

"I don't have any of the details. Mom just told me he died on a special ops mission in Iraq trying to assassinate Saddam Hussein. She always changes the subject. I don't like to press her because I don't want to upset her."

"That's normal. But it leaves you wondering, doesn't it?"

"Wondering?" Mira asked. She looked over at the old man. His eyes still faced forward, but now they brimmed with tears.

"Are you all right?" she asked.

He paused while he watched the Amazon people walking in and out of the Spheres.

"It's all these young folks walking by. So many of them dead-eyed. That's what I call it: dead-eyed. Maybe that's why they like those zombie movies so much. You know, the walking dead people?

"In my life, I've seen the worst of it. I saw my best friend standing next to me one minute go off to take a piss, and the next minute seen the top of his head blown off while he was walkin back to us. He dropped right there in his tracks, eyes wide open with the most puzzled look on his face like 'what the fuck just happened?' We didn't even hear the round that got him.

"My freshman year in high school, I watched the newscast film of Jack Kennedy's head fly open, just like my friend's, ridin in the back of his limo while Jackie jumped over him to shield him. Four years later, we saw live pictures of Bobby Kennedy lying on the floor of the hotel kitchen with his lifeblood flowin out of him. It scared me out of my wits, and I thought the world was comin apart, and then just ten months later came the pictures of Martin Luther King slumped on the deck outside his motel room, with all his friends pointing up to where the bullet came from. After I got back from Nam, I got to watch Richard Nixon lie his fucking ass off and flash a double peace sign when he got on his helicopter and got his ass out of town without goin to jail, that fuckin asshole. I wanted to kill that fucker for what he did to our country—my country, the country we went and died for.

"And even after seeing all I've seen in my seventy years, all the pain and turmoil and violence, I never wanted to be no zombie. I never wanted to go brain-dead and look at the world through dead eyes. I never wanted to walk around with my head down, eyes to the ground, not sayin hello, and good-day, and how-are-you-doin to people.

"And I sure as hell never want to miss an opportunity to sit on a bench on a beautiful day like today havin a proper conversation with a beautiful brown woman like you. You are some-thin special, you are. I want to thank you for taking the time to sit down next to me. I want to thank you for taking the time to see me and talk to me. And thank you for being a human being and treating me like a human being, for not being a dead-eyed zombie."

Mira went mute. All she could do was slide her hand across the seat of the bench and softly cover his. Before he could protest, she leaned over and gently kissed his cheek. As she withdrew, he reached his other hand up to cover the kiss and permanently affix it to his face. Mira stood, and, for a moment, their eyes met once more, live eyes to live eyes, before she turned to walk the short few blocks to her office.

As she walked, Mira reached her left hand into her purse, deftly popped the cap off her pill bottle without withdrawing it, fished out two oxys, slipped them between her lips, and pulverized them with her teeth.

| 6 |

Mira never used oxys at work—it was a rule. Maybe a little legal cannabis in her vape when she went out on break, or a THC gummy or two when she felt a little tense and under deadline. But that was medicinal, and everyone did it. This morning was different. The talk outside the Spheres rattled her, and she'd popped the oxys without thinking.

Back in her office, Mira stared at the names of the 6,828 Americans who died in Afghanistan and Iraq as they scrolled over the screen of her computer. She'd entered her father's name into the search field and froze when the screen reported "no results." After sitting for what might have been two minutes or perhaps twenty, she got up and walked into the bathroom. She peered into the face in the mirror. Dead eyes peered back at her. She felt nothing.

Mira returned to her desk and IM'd her manager that she was sick and needed to go home. She walked out the front door, circled back by the Spheres, but found the bench deserted. Making her way south on Western Avenue, Mira looked into the eyes of a few of the young people coming toward her sporting their Amazon badges around their necks. She gave them a plastic smile and a half-hearted, "Hello, how are you today?" as they passed by. Most looked down at their feet; some mumbled a few indecipherable syllables; others looked at her as if she were from another planet. Since her talk with the old man, she realized how few humans inhabited the downtown Seattle landscape now.

Mira hoped Ian was home when she got there—she needed a hug, but when she walked through the front door, the condo was quiet and bare. The oxys had worn off, and she didn't have any kratom, so she was crashing into a deeper depression. She needed something to keep her from going any lower and knew Ian kept his coke in two glass vials rolled up in a pair of his socks in the top drawer of his dresser. She grabbed one vial, tapped out a small pile on top of the dresser, cut it into two precise lines, and quickly inhaled them up each nostril. The euphoria was immediate and intense. She raised her head to peer into the eyes looking back at her from the mirror above the dresser. "Shit!"

Feeling the familiar dizziness of an erupting panic attack, she went into the bathroom and drew a hot bath, throwing in her favorite lavender bath salts. While the bath filled, she stripped naked and, unable to distract herself from the stabbing barrage of anxiety, spent a few minutes on her bed, playing with her favorite mini vibrator and some intimate body cream. When the tub had filled, she padded naked into the kitchen, filled a glass full of Merlot, lit a vanilla candle, then returned to the bathroom and lowered herself into the hot, lavender-laced water.

After two deep draws of Merlot, paired with the warmth of the water, her muscles loosened. She closed her eyes and imagined the morass of thinking that pinballed through her cluttered mind dissolving like the lavender bath salts into her steamy bathwater. She longed for her mind to release her—the drugs in her system, along with the alcohol, made for a cocktail of mental confusion.

Mira leaned back as her muscles softened. The natural weight of her body started it sliding down into the water. Her consciousness began slipping downward with it into another realm, another place, sliding into an ancient time, yet concurrent. Now, her naked body rested peacefully in a pool of hot mineral water under a black night sky among the tall trees of a tropical forest. Long, fine hair covered her dark skin and floated alongside her on the surface of the water. Her naïve eyes fell upon the small motionless form she had just pushed from her body that floated next to her. Mira felt confused and angry. Why is she now in this other place, outside in a pool of warm water, with tall trees standing beside her, this small being floating lifelessly beside her? Why? Terror gripped her.

One by one, Mira's chin, mouth, nose, eyes, hair, and finally, the top of her head submerged. The warm liquid surrounded every inch of her, embraced her and enveloped her in complete bliss. She waited only for the water to fill her lungs so she could feel the completeness of its caress from within and without. She was ready.

From a distance, she heard her own voice silently whisper, "Please take me now; I don't want to do this anymore."

| 7 |

"Mira! Mira! What the fuck are you doing?"

Strong hands pulled her limp body out of the tub and onto the bathmat.

"I'm fine! What the fuck are you doing? Leave me alone!" she protested. "I'm just taking a bath."

Mira picked herself off the bathroom floor, wrapped herself in a towel, and stalked into the bedroom with Ian following close behind.

"Your eyes were wide open, and you were under the fucking water on the bottom of the tub. I thought you were fucking dead!" Ian shrieked.

"I was trying to relax. I had a panic attack."

"Then why did you use coke? I found the vial and razor blade on top of my dresser before I found you in the bathroom. You scared the shit out of me."

"Because I came home depressed, and you weren't here. I thought some coke would help."

Mira's conflicted report muddled Ian's concrete brain. "How can you be depressed and have a panic attack at the same time?" he said.

"I talked with a Vietnam vet outside the Spheres about losing my dad in the war and felt depressed, so I took some oxys. Then I couldn't work and came home hoping you were here and could hug me and you weren't here. I thought the coke would help the depression, but I started having a panic attack after I snorted it. Once the panic attack started, I didn't know what to do, so I decided a glass of wine and a hot bath with bath salts would help."

She decided not to tell him about the vibrator.

She waited for Ian to respond when she noticed he had stopped blinking, so she continued.

"I submerged myself because it felt good."

She also didn't tell him about the vision or the voice in her head and what it'd said while she lay underwater.

"I've got a gig tonight and really can't do this right now," he said. "Why don't you try to sleep off all the shit you've got rolling around inside, and maybe we can make some sense of this tomorrow?"

Ian's suggestion was a good one. Most of the drugs had worn off, and Mira felt exhausted. The events of the day, along with the residue of the drugs metabolizing in Mira's cells, stirred in her subconscious mind as she slipped into unconsciousness. She fell into a deep sleep lying on top of her comforter, still wrapped in the towel she'd grabbed. She didn't hear him leave the condo.

~

Mira entered a vivid dream in the depth of her sleep—one that hadn't come to her before, or perhaps it had. The illusion began in her body without visual or lucid content. First, a pleas.ing sensation of excitement arose in her arms. The depression and panic finally left her. But, as she moved deeper into the dream, she realized that the arms she felt were not her own but the arms of another. She inhabited a different body.

Then, a sharp, pungent smell pierced her nostrils. Screams assaulted her ears. Smoke encircled her. Through the smoke, a scene of chaos and death came into focus. Unbelievable death. The body she inhabited vibrated with fear and excitement. A killing field of war surrounded her. She held a long gun in her arms—a rifle tipped with a long, slender blade. She ran break.neck through the field, screaming as she raced into a battle packed with soldiers clad in blue and gray uniforms, fighting shoulder to shoulder.

She looked down at her gray Confederate uniform and male body. This Rebel soldier's body felt euphoric, high on the prospect of killing those fucking Yankees. As he raced ahead, he thrust his blade through the first body in front of him, withdrawing it just as quickly, making his instrument of death ready for his next victim. The Union soldier he killed collapsed onto the soft grass below. He felt no compassion, no regret, no humanity as he advanced. He saw no human faces on the bodies he pierced. If he perceived a single face on a single body, glimpsed a bit of fear, pain, or regret, he might feel the emotions of his act, which would be unbearable. These were not human beings; they were the enemy, and he must defeat and destroy them. These people meant to steal his God-given rights away from him: the right to own his property, his land, and his slaves. They intended to steal this Confederate's control over his women and animals, his right to do whatever he damn well pleased, no matter what effect it had on others.

Damn these weak, bleeding-heart Yankees, she thought in her Confederate body. Damn them all to hell! He wanted them all to die, and then he wanted to die himself to protect his rights and beliefs. Come and get me if you can, you fuckers. I'll take as many of you to hell with me as I can!

~

Mira awoke from the dream drenched in sweat. She went into the bathroom shaken and sat on the toilet to pee. As she calmed down, the conscious memory of the dream slipped away. When she awoke the next morning, the dream had returned safely to the depth of her subconscious mind. The attempted information download would wait for another opportunity for processing.

| 8 |

Mira decided that a road trip might shake her out of her malaise, so she joined her old university friends for their annual week-long pilgrimage to Whistler. The invitation couldn't have come at a better time.

Whistler Blackcomb, British Columbia, north of the Canadian border in the Canadian Cascade Mountain Range, had always been a destination for avid skiers. Now, it had become a playground for the money-fueled millennials who populated the insane explosion of the Seattle tech boom. During the seventies, the baby boomers who came to Whistler were Deadheads and hippies looking to get high and ski. Back then, cheap ski cabins and funky places to eat dotted the mountain village. Visitors brought the homegrown weed they grew in backyard gardens and large indoor planters. It was weak but effective. They used water-filled bongs or rolled joints to get high. They knew it was dangerous to cross the Canadian border with stashes large enough for sale, but small amounts for personal use hidden in nooks and crannies of cars made it through safely most of the time. When border patrol agents discovered visitors' stashes, the baggies or boxes usually disap-peared without consequence, lost to the officers who pocketed the contraband for their personal use.

Boomers liked their LSD made up as blotter acid: drops of the potent liquid dripped onto tiny squares of super-light tissue paper designed to melt on their tongue, or cubes of sugar that dissolved in their mouths. The potent drug sent them into an in-tense six-to eight-hour trip, complete with melting walls and distorted faces. Strength and dosing varied, and people rarely knew what they'd bought or passed around.

The new breed of tech millennials traveling from Seattle to Whistler to enjoy skiing in the winter and hiking and backpacking in the summer preferred alcohol, cannabis, and prescription drugs. In their baggage, they stashed the oxys, fentanyl, Adder-all, Ritalin, Valium, and Xanax they'd picked up easily on the street or through prescriptions from willing doc-tors. Alcohol flowed freely in the growing selection of bars and clubs that proliferated in the modern-day Whistler village. After Washington State and Canada legalized cannabis, the stress of bringing it across the border became unnecessary. Blotter acid was readily available and easy to transport, and vacationers knew how to micro-dose to control the length and intensity of a trip.

Mira and her friends enjoyed the ability to ski, shop, club, and dine at the new upscale Whistler. They mixed their cannabis edibles with skiing during the day—perhaps not the safest idea—then showered quickly and dressed in sexy party clothes for a quick turnaround into the active nightlife, hitting the upscale clubs and music venues the village had to offer. Alcohol and drugs flowed freely, and hardly anyone returned to their room alone.

But, on the very first day of her much-needed getaway, fate stepped in and sent Mira on a trip she never expected. Her friends picked her up early Saturday morning for the four-and-a-half-hour drive to the resort. With an hour-long wait at the border and delays checking in, it was 4:00 p.m. by the time they settled into their rooms. The group changed to hit the slopes for some late-afternoon runs before dinner, and even though the trip had exhausted her, Mira went along with the plan.

Her friends called her a klutz, and she never really enjoyed the athletics of skiing. She skied more to fit in than for the love of the sport. So on this day, and this run, as she turned her head to witness her friend Amanda whizzing past her while taking a video of herself on her iPhone, Mira broke up laughing uncontrollably. The tips of her skis crossed and sent her tumbling head over heels into a violent fall. Her body twisted counterclockwise in a somersault through the air before colliding into the hard-packed snow of the ski run. The airborne twist, combined with her ski-binding jamming when she hit the ground, created too much force for her leg to endure, and while her femur absorbed and flexed through the torque of the twist, her tibia couldn't bear it and suffered a devastating displaced spiral fracture.

A bolt of white-hot lightning shot up her left leg as the loud snap of bone separating from itself vaulted her into maximum shock. When she finally skidded to a stop, the sight of the nub of milky-white bone that poked through the light-blue polyester of her ski pants and the blot of deep-crimson-red liquid growing around it caused her to vomit onto the cold snow her cheek rested on. Then, the sight of her own bone and blood catapulted her directly out of her body and into black unconsciousness.

| 9 |

The faded pink frame of the used sixteen-inch bike between Mira's skinny legs seemed giant and wobbly. Her muscles possessed no memory of balancing on a two-wheeled moving object, so she struggled to keep her feet on the thick pedals, manage the handlebars, and still keep from falling over sideways.

Why do I need to learn how to ride a bike, anyway? she silently whined to herself. Part of her felt like she'd die, and part of her felt excited and powerful. A strong massive hand guided her from behind, half holding onto the seat she sat on and half on the small of her butt. Her father's familiar and loving presence and the touch of his hand calmed her and gave her courage. Her small hands gripped the handlebar ends tightly while she continued to hear the reassuring sound of his steady footsteps jogging along behind her. She pushed the pedals first with her left foot, then with her right.

His deep voice vibrated behind her, soothing her right to her core. "You can do this, Mira; you can do this." She felt her muscles release from the tension they'd been holding.

"I know you can do it, Mira. Just relax and have

fun. Your body already knows how to balance itself. It learned balance when you started walking. Just let it do what it already knows. Keep pedaling and relax your hands on the handle grips. Breathe right into your seat and imagine your entire body flowing, just like the stream behind our house. You're doing it!"

Mira felt her father's love filling her heart and didn't notice when his hand separated from her back. The steady sound of his footsteps faded behind her unnoticed. She giggled and pedaled by herself all the way down the alleyway, where she finally lost control and crashed into an empty trash can next to a neighbor's garage. She fell in a tangled heap with her bike and heard her own laughter as it echoed back up the alleyway. Her eyes searched in vain to once more glimpse the face, feel the touch, and hear the deep voice that had guided her.

"Mira . . . Mira; can you hear me? Mira . . . try to wake up," an unknown voice urged.

But Mira's eyes didn't obey. Her body went numb, and yet every square inch of it hurt. Her eyelids finally parted a bit and allowed her to focus enough to see through the fog. She glimpsed her left leg peeking out from under the flimsy cotton of a hospital gown. It hung cradled in a sling suspended from the bland-green ceiling above her. She rolled her head to the right and encountered a light-blue video screen displaying red, white, and green graphs and numbers, but they spoke gibberish. Her gaze traveled slowly to the left to follow a length of clear, thin vinyl tubing that emerged from a plastic bag hanging on an IV stand—just like Mira had seen in hospital movies. A clear liquid made its way down the tube as it snaked its path to a needle that disappeared deep into a vein on the back of Mira's right hand. Trimmed white medical tape secured the needle to her skin.

"Where am I?" Mira croaked.

She hadn't noticed the young man wearing a starched-white, knee-length lab coat over crisp purple scrubs, writing notes in a stainless-steel patient-chart holder as he leaned against the far wall of the room. His skin was deep tan, and his slicked-down straight hair was jet black. She couldn't make out the tough name displayed on the name tag pinned to his lapel, but the M period D period was clear.

Startled, he looked up and spoke in a heavily accented, clinical-sounding monotone. "You are in the Harborview Hospital Trauma Unit in Seattle, Washington. Your medical insurance paid for an ambulance helicopter to transport you here from Canada. You've suffered a compound spiral fracture of the left tibia. That is a serious injury. It means the fracture separated the bone from itself in a spiral break, and part of the bone penetrated the outer skin of your leg."

Mira scanned his eyes for a glimmer of emotion or empathy without satisfaction.

Vague images of the tumbling fall crept back into Mira's drug-fogged memory as the doctor delivered his monotone orthopedic lecture. The scarlet-red pool of blood spreading from the stark white of bone protruding through her ski pants came back to her consciousness. She gagged, but nothing came up, metallic nausea remaining trapped in her stomach.

His droning continued, "Because of the serious-ness of your injury, they placed your leg in an air cast and airlifted you from Whistler to Vancouver and then on to Seattle. We've kept you heavily sedated with fentanyl to get you home. The accident happened yesterday morning."

"Yesterday morning," Mira mumbled. "I don't even know what year it is." She thought she might be in a dream, living someone else's life. And then she passed out again.

Mira moved in and out of consciousness for several days while the doctors performed three sep-arate surgeries, trying to cobble her shattered leg back together. General anesthesia, followed by heavy doses of pain medication, left her in a semiconscious netherworld of hazy images filled with carnage and death, confusing reality with delusion. Warriors lay broken, bleeding, and dying, piled on top of each other on grassy fields of battle. She wandered naked and aimless among the bodies. Her bare feet slipped on and sank into the blood-soaked soil, the earth irrep-arably stained crimson red. The smell of charred and dying flesh assaulted her nostrils, her bare skin irri-tated by the smoke of black powder. She picked her way through the carnage, stepping over and around body parts separated from bodies. As she wandered the field, she stumbled over a tiny human form and looked down. A baby lay on the ground at her feet, crying out for its mother. Why don't I feel anything? Should I pick it up? Try to find its mother? What should I do?

A chorus of moans mixed with screams filled her ears. Feeling numb and detached, she stepped over the baby and picked her way among the dead and dying. They cried out to her and reached their arms up to her for help. Why am I here? What am I supposed to do? Please, someone, answer me!

Off in the distance, bright strands of navy blue and neon green pierced the night sky, glowing atop tall, slender crane-like structures that turned slowly left and right. Stumbling onto a dirt road deeply rutted by wagon wheels that had born heavy cannons of war, she paused to look at the object she carried in her left hand. Peering at its glowing surface, she pressed a symbol displayed there. When the familiar map appeared, she automatically called for a black car at her location and tapped "home" for her destination. Within seconds, a large sedan pulled up beside her. She popped the small white orb she held in her hand into her mouth, crunched it between her teeth, slid onto the soft leather of the seat, and descended into oblivion.

| 10 |

Mira improved remarkably following her surgeries. She remained in the rehab department at Harborview, receiving physical therapy for two weeks before being transferred to the Virginia Mason Sports Medicine Rehab Center for a month of treatment and physical therapy. Amazon provided their employees with excellent health insurance, so Mira received the highest level of care available. They brought her meals and snacks, the TV had every movie channel available, the internet connection was blazing fast, and her physical therapy included regular massage therapy and hydrotherapy. In addition, she received disability insurance at a rate of 80 percent of her salary.

Her medical records showed no evidence of drug overuse or abuse, so her doctors put no restrictions on her pain medications. Her formulary included OxyContin and fentanyl available to her at her discretion. She experienced a great deal of pain throughout her recovery and required regular dosing to stay "ahead of the pain," as her doctors advised. But Mira always added a point or two on her "pain scale" just for good measure and stashed doses away for safekeeping.

During Mira's hospital and rehab stay, Ian's visits became less frequent, and he didn't stay long at each visit. Mira excused his absence, attributing it to the loss of having sex with her. Between the recovery pain she experienced and the opioids she took, her libido dropped to zero. She was glad he wasn't around bugging her for sex. She planned to take care of what he wanted once she got home. Visits from the friends who'd accompanied her to Whistler kept her spirits up.

The day before her transfer to the rehab center, Mira was sitting up in bed reading Stephen King and didn't notice her come into the room.

"Hi, Mir," she whispered.

Only one person called her Mir, and she always hated it. Mira looked up to see her mother standing motionless just inside the door. She hadn't visited since the accident—not surprising given the distance that had developed between them. The last time Mira saw Gina, she had invited her to a Thanksgiving dinner she tried to host. Was it three years ago or four? Grandma Nona always hosted Thanksgiving when she was alive, so her mother trying to pull it off had been a disaster, especially with Sergei present.

Gina remained framed in the doorway, silent and still for what seemed like five minutes. Extra lines creased her face, and the circles under her eyes had darkened since the last time Mira had seen her. Familiar butterflies fluttered about Mira's stomach. Would she ever get over the man her mother had brought home to be her stepfather when she was seven years old?

"What's up, Mom?" Mira asked with a chill.

"I heard about the accident from Brian," Gina replied.

Brian was Mira's best friend in high school. Mira had figured out that Brian was gay before he knew it himself, and he loved her for accepting him just the way he was. They would be friends for life. He knew about the cut-off between Mira and her mother, so Brian kept Gina informed about important events in Mira's life.

"I knew an engraved invitation to see you wouldn't be coming, so I came by anyway."

The butterflies grew into bumblebees with every sarcastic word her mother uttered.

"There's something I need to tell you. It's been a secret too long," Gina continued without pausing. "I came to tell you that your father is alive."

Without noticing, Mira stopped breathing.

~

Mira had been a classic latchkey kid. From the time she was three months old, her mother had left her at a private neighborhood daycare home down the street. With her father off on deployment for months at a time, and her mother preferring to work rather than stay at home with her, Mira spent her earliest days in the paneled basement playroom of the day-care home. The little ones lolled about in playpens, entertaining themselves with simple toys or napping until their parents came to pick them up. Then, when they were big enough to move and walk, they spent most days in the side room, playing with each other or sitting alone. Lunch was in the large kitchen upstairs and always the same: peanut butter and jelly sandwiches, paper cups of orange juice, and carrot and celery sticks to dip in ranch dressing. It never changed.

By the time she was six and in first grade, Mira walked alone the three blocks from school to home, rustling up her own after-school snack, then watching TV or playing Nintendo until her mother returned from work. Gina worked full-time as a loan officer at the neighborhood branch of the Bank of America and spent most of her weekends with an unknown man she met somewhere. Her staunch Catholic upbringing was no match for the white-hot Italian blood running through her, and although her mother had given her the name Teresa, she was not a saint. She went by Gina.

Gina wanted her weekends to herself, so she dropped Mira off at her mother's house across town. Mira loved her time with her "Nona" Rose, and Nona loved having her around. Her grandmother was gentle and loving, and although she wore a heavy dose of perfume, Mira loved her scent. Sadly, Nona's husband had died in a construction accident, and she'd never remarried. Gina was just three when her father died, and her memories of him existed only in pictures.

When Nona Rose lost her mate, she lost the love of her life. He proved irreplaceable. Mira never met him, and Gina never spoke of him, but Nona did. Nona had colorized the faded black-and-white photo of him in his crisp Army uniform that looked out from an antique pewter picture frame. She'd carefully placed it on a handmade lace doily atop the end table next to her aging sofa. All she would say about him was that he served in the Army Corp of Engineers during the Korean War and stayed in the army until Rose was old enough to marry him. She said he had the most romantic Italian accent she'd ever heard but said nothing about his family.

Rose told Mira that soon after they married and just before Gina was born, they'd ventured out to California. San Francisco was looking for experienced tunnel engineers to work on a new underwater rail tunnel they were building from San Francisco to Oakland. Barak had tunnel experience both in New York and in the army, so they quickly grabbed him and moved the entire family to California.

The picture showed off Barak's Italian good looks, complete with piercing, transparent blue eyes. Nona still teared up when she spoke of their love for one another and their abbreviated time together. In an identical pewter frame, an unretouched faded sepia picture of Nona's mother, Miriam, sat on an identical lace doily. Miriam had passed away from breast cancer that she refused to have treated five years before Gina was born. When Gina became pregnant and gave birth to a girl, Rose asked Gina to name her in memory of her mother. Gina wasn't fond of Miriam's given name, but she enjoyed honoring the grandmother she'd never met and agreed to shorten it to Mira.

On those weekends when Gina left Mira with

her Nona Rose, they always started with the same ritual. First, Nona pulled her favorite black-vinyl LP record out of its pristine case and carefully laid the disk onto her ancient Sony record player with its speakers detached and spread out on her dining room sideboard. Then they both listened to Louis Armstrong's throaty voice:

> I see skies of blue
> and clouds of white,
> the bright blessed day,
> the dark sacred night.
> And I think to myself,
> What a wonderful world.

Nona sat Mira down on a stool in the kitchen, brushed her long, thick, natural-ginger-red hair down her back for what seemed like hours, then carefully trimmed off the last half-inch of frizzed ends. Following that, she carefully separated her locks into two equal sides with a perfect part down the middle, then used her index and middle finger to divide each side into three equal parts all the way from her scalp. Carefully, she first laid the right lock over the middle lock to the left, then the left lock over the middle lock to the right, and continued the process to the bottom until she created a perfectly formed braid that she topped off with a rubber band binding the end. Then she moved to the other side of Mira's head and repeated the ritual until a pure-white perfectly straight line of scalp traced from Mira's forehead over her crown all the way to the top of her nape until she had braided every single hair on Mira's head into two perfect red weaves that formed mirror images of each other. As she worked, the two talked nonstop about everything under the sun, but Nona never mentioned Mira's father, and Mira never asked.

Whenever Mira asked her mother about her father, Gina told her he was a Green Beret killed on a special op mission tracking down the Iraqi dictator Saddam Hussein. The story never varied, and Gina offered no specifics. Mira heard she could check the Killed-and-Missing-in-Action lists the government published, but she never did. Instead, Gina had explained that the operation was a secret and that they sealed the records of his death. Deep in her gut, Mira didn't believe her mother but never questioned her. It seemed like a perfectly acceptable explanation for why her father wasn't with them rather than any other story she might make up herself.

~

"Didn't you hear me? I just told you your father is alive," Gina practically yelled. Mira's breathing resumed, and her attention returned to the present. "Alive? Why didn't you tell me before this?"

"That's not important now. I'm afraid he doesn't have much time left, and I couldn't keep it a secret any longer. He's in the VA in Portland. He has cirrhosis and lung cancer. I've seen him, and he doesn't have much time."

The walls of Mira's room contracted, and her chest tightened. She gulped for air. Stiletto-sharp anger rose from her gut into her throat. She wished her mother dead. But when she looked up from her bed and into Gina's eyes, she saw the deep pain and sorrow that inhabited her. The weight of Gina's secret had etched into the pale skin of her face. Guilt and shame lowered her shoulders and head. Her gaze dropped to the floor. When Mira saw how fragile Gina looked, her anger lifted like the fog over Elliott Bay. She became six again.

"Can I see him?" she asked in a small voice.

"He asks for you constantly," Gina said, sobbing. "I told him I didn't know how you would react. I'm so sorry, Mira."

Mira reached her hands toward her mother, and Gina collapsed onto the bed next to her, their arms intertwined. They cried there together—two little girls who'd both lost their fathers far too young.

| 11 |

With her rehab progressing well, Mira couldn't wait to visit her father. The doctors replaced her full-leg cast with a lower-leg cast from just below her knee to just above her ankle. The leg scooter and foot boot they provided allowed her to move about easily. She believed she could safely take the train down to Portland, reconnect with her father, and come straight home to her condo to get back to her relationship and job.

She'd grown accustomed to the pleasure of the fentanyl they'd prescribed her. Although the pain would have been manageable with OxyContin and anti-inflammatories, she convinced the doctors to keep her on the stronger narcotics for the time being. She often took half doses and stashed the extras for later. The drug dulled her emotions along with her physical pain, and she appreciated that side effect. Her happy pills soothed the stress of the intense emotions she felt while planning to meet the father she'd believed dead and hadn't seen since age six.

Mira always loved the train ride from Seattle to Portland. She treasured the beauty and time to be alone. The trip began at the King Street Train Station just south of downtown. Mira loved the iconic twelve-story clock tower rising above the roof, and the terra-cotta and marble surfaces reminiscent of old Venice that drenched the interior. Before leaving, she would stand for a few minutes under the four-story vaulted compass rotunda, looking upward until she became dizzy.

The train ride to Portland initially follows the coast of Puget Sound as it moves south to Tacoma. Then it crosses over the trestle at the Cowlitz River as it flows into the Columbia River near Longview, north of Portland. As an avid reader, the Kindle app on Mira's iPad Mini contained a carefully selected collection of over 500 novels. Her favorite author was Patricia Cornwell, who wrote the Kay Scarpetta series. The author's principal character is a forensic medical examiner who solved murders by getting herself involved in the action herself. Mira loved imagining herself solving complex murder cases. When the gore of Scarpetta's autopsies got too much for her, and Mira needed a lighter comedic read, she turned to Janet Evanovich's character Stephanie Plum, an unlikely bounty hunter cruising around in her grandmother's 1953 Buick Roadmaster—dubbed "Big Blue"—finding bail jumpers and bringing them back in to collect the bounty. Under normal circumstances, Mira would have enjoyed the train ride, alternately reading her novels and taking breaks to enjoy the beauty of the passing countryside even on a grey, rainy Northwest day. But these were not normal circumstances.

Just one fentanyl provided Mira a relaxed and

pleasant ride down, but as she departed the train and slipped into an Uber for the quick trip to the Portland VA Medical Center, an intense mix of emotions rose in her. She bit off another half of one of her pills, crunching it into powder and holding it under her tongue until it dissolved into her bloodstream. She was used to the bitter medicinal taste in her mouth, and the effect was immediate. When she arrived, the driver helped get her leg-scooter out of the trunk, and she wheeled herself into the stark lobby of the hospital.

"Martin Washington's room, please," Mira said to the disinterested receptionist. Without a word, the woman handed her a slip of paper that bore the number 2102. Mira rolled onto the elevator and departed on the second floor. Taking a deep breath, she propelled herself down the hall to the door bearing the number 2102. Her heart seemed to be beating outside her chest. Sweat broke from her palms, wetting her clenched fists, but she pushed through the weight of the heavy hospital door, knowing she could wait no longer.

She stood motionless just inside the door. Heavy drapes masked the bright sun of the Portland afternoon. He was dozing in the semi-darkness. She waited for her eyes to adjust and bring the form lying on the hospital bed into focus. His frail body barely tented the bed covers. A cotton hospital skullcap shrouded his hairless scalp, attempting to contain his vital body warmth. His head rested with his brow lightly furrowed on the starched cover of his pillow, and his drawn features peeked out between the top of his blanket and his skullcap. With his covers pulled tight, it appeared as if he was simply a head placed upon a platter. Mira had no conscious memory of his complexion, and his African skin tone was deeper than she'd imagined. His deep skin color belied his Slave Coast ancestry and reflected their shared DNA, which Mira showed in her luscious copper complexion.

She gazed for several moments before she could find her voice again. "Dad?" Her voice cracked. "Dad?" she repeated, firmer this time.

Slowly, his lids slit open. Blood-red vessels on the surface of his eyes surrounded black irises. A few clouds of cataracts showed through. He said nothing.

Mira walked over to the windows and pulled back the curtains. Sunlight flooded into the room, illuminating his form and hers.

"Mira? Is that you, Mira? Is it really you, or have I died and gone to heaven?"

There was the voice! It was much weaker, but the tone and timbre were unmistakable. In an instant, the sound of his voice transported Mira back onto her faded-pink bike. She felt his firm hand on her butt as he held onto the seat, balancing her as she pedaled. His deep voice guided and reassured her. The speech she'd rehearsed so many times for this long-awaited meeting dissolved into oblivion as her heart cracked wide open. Her voice failed her.

"What did you do to those amazing red locks of yours?" he asked.

Mira was not yet privy to the secrets of her maternal ancestry—history Nona Rose had kept hidden. She'd told Gina that her parents were a classic mix of Italian Catholic and Irish Catholic ancestry. Nona sported curly ginger hair, but a quirk of genetics is that red hair is a gene that can pop up without warning, so the secret of Mira's ancestry remained dormant.

Growing up, Mira had hated her thick red hair —it didn't match with her confusing skin tones, and when she'd had the chance, she'd done everything in her power to change it. Finally, when she was eleven years old, she shoplifted a box of hair dye from the drugstore and had practically destroyed the bathroom and several towels, dying her hair black.

"You remember my hair?" Mira said in a squeaky voice.

"I remember everything about you."

"Why did you leave me?"

Martin looked out the window, gathering his feelings and thoughts as he struggled to fight down his guilt and shame. He finally replied, though unable to look her in the eyes. "I don't want to make excuses, Mira."

"But I need to hear what happened," she said. "Mom lied to me and said you were dead. Why did she do that?"

His gaze moved from the window to the floor. "She didn't lie; I asked her to," he whispered.

Mira spoke louder. "Then tell me what happened."

Martin gazed out the window as he began his

story. "You were about five years old when the Gulf War started. I was a career sergeant in special ops for the US Army. We were on a secret mission embedded with the Iraqi forces to take out Saddam Hussein. The day after I arrived there, a firefight broke out, and I got hit by a 50-caliber round." His eyes went hard, and his gaze drifted to the corner of the room as he reentered the reality of his past:

Dressed in special-op battle fatigues and the high-tech gear of war, Sargent Martin Washington patrolled a deserted town with his squad about ten clicks outside Fallujah, Iraq. An advanced combat helmet with communications equipment encased his head, while heavy body armor enveloped his torso. Belts of ammunition for his field rifle encircled his chest, along with a first-aid kit, water bottles, and a complement of grenades. A Glock 19 perched on his hip belt, with six extra-high-capacity clips close by. Cradled in his arms and across his chest lay his Mk12 special-purpose rifle. He felt every bit of the sixty pounds of extra weight he carried, but his training and conditioning bore the burden easily. His advanced mental training erased any trace of fear from his mind and body. They'd made him a machine of war, an expert at his craft. He was on patrol, and nothing else existed.

His robotic eyes rotated back and forth, scanning the doorways and alleyways for the enemy. But, this time, a young woman with loving eyes and brown skin stood watching him in a doorway off to the right. She seemed familiar, but he felt unsure. His heart fluttered. He raised his carbine, sighted a red dot on her chest, and tensed his left index finger on the trigger.

An unknown female voice from inside of him interrupted and said,

"No."

And then his hip exploded as the round slammed into him.

Panic gripped his body, and, in slow motion, he collapsed onto the cobblestone path below.

Terror flooded his body from every firefight and every patrol in which he'd taken part. Every enemy combatant he'd ever shot flashed in front of his eyes. Contorted faces of every human being he'd slain in hand-to-hand combat appeared and vanished in quick succession. His soul shattered as each act of war he'd ever committed flooded his memory. He felt awash in guilt and shame. Finally, in the presence and the witness of this pure young woman, this daughter he'd left behind, he faced what he'd done. And then he returned to his hospital bed.

"Oh God, Mira, I'm so ashamed. I should never have left you and Gina. My life was with you guys, not off fighting someone else's war. I know that now, and there's nothing I can do about it."

"Tell me the rest, Dad. I want to hear it all," Mira said through her tears.

"Hardly anyone survives that kind of wound, but I did. They hospitalized me for over a year, and I had twelve different surgeries. I lost a kidney, my spleen, part of my liver, and part of my large intestine. The round destroyed my hip, and, even after all the surgeries, I needed arm crutches to walk."

Mira fought back the waves of nausea that washed over her as her father, emotionless, told his story.

"They gave me straight morphine to manage the pain, and half the time, I was out of my mind. I was in complete survival mode. The only thing keeping me going was thinking about you and Gina. I wanted to make it back to you."

Mira realized she'd never heard her mother's name spoken aloud from her father's mouth. Grief-laden tears rolled down her face.

"They transferred me to Walter Reed, and Gina came to see me a few times. I really wasn't a man anymore. There was no way I could function as a husband and father. I knew I would be a burden on you both and weigh you down. The army put me up as an outpatient for a lifetime of rehab and weaned me off the morphine. But I was already hooked, and street heroin was just as good. My general health was shot, and I knew I'd never recover. There was no way I would grow old and hold my grandchildren. So, on what would be her last visit, I told Gina not to come back and not to contact me. She cried like a baby and said she wanted me to come home anyway, but I knew she couldn't handle it, and I said no. I told her to forget about me and to tell you I was dead. You both deserved a whole man, and I was not even half one. That was the last time I saw her until she told me about your accident." Tears filled his eyes.

"You knew about my accident?"

"She called and told me. At first, I wouldn't answer when I saw her caller ID. She tried to reach me every day, but I never answered. Finally, I decided it would be best for everyone if she forgot about me. I figured your memories of me would fade away. Finally, she gave up and stopped calling. At that point, I felt like I'd died." His tears broke free, cascading down his cheeks. He turned to wipe them away.

After he composed himself, he continued, "She didn't know I kept stalking her on Facebook, so I knew she married some Russian guy. That's how I kept up on you, too. I'm ashamed of it, but I've been watching you from a distance on Facebook ever since I learned how to do it. When Gina called me about your accident, she told me I was an idiot and a fool and said she wouldn't play by my rules anymore. That's when I told her about my cancer and that I had little time. I was refusing treatment so I could finally make the story real about dying in the war.

"She told me she visited you in the hospital and told you I was still alive. It was as if breaking your leg willed us back together. I might be only half a man in my eyes, but I thought I might still be a whole father in yours, and it wasn't right for me to cheat you out of that any longer. Since your accident, they did surgery to remove the tumors and chemo to keep them from spreading. But I waited too long, and it's spread to my pancreas and lungs."

Tears streamed down Mira's face, drenching her shirt. She climbed into bed next to her father, buried her face in his chest, and sobbed for what must've been an hour while he held her close. Mira listened to the faint heartbeat she hadn't heard in so long, trying to live the thirty years she'd lost in the minutes and hours she had left. "I'm staying here with you, Dad . . . I'm staying."

| 12 |

When she left the VA that night, Mira found an Airbnb close to the hospital that allowed unlimited stays. It had a pleasant kitchen, bathroom, and washer and dryer, so she stocked it with nutritious food and the personal items she'd need for an extended stay. Mira vowed to be with her father until he breathed his last breath. It would be hard, and she'd never been with anyone when they died, but she knew she must. She'd come straight from the rehab center, so she still had her suitcase from her original trip to Whistler. The Airbnb included a washer and dryer, and she could walk to a physical therapy clinic close by. Walgreens had her fentanyl prescription in their system, and, for now, she'd convinced the doctors she could handle unlimited refills on a scheduled basis.

She called her manager at Amazon to let her know what was going on, and they accommodated her with a grant of family and medical leave of up to three months if she needed it. She wanted to do a little work to stay connected and have some distraction from the intensity of her recovery and her father's impending death. Her manager gave her permission to work remotely one or two projects at her own pace.

After that, she was free to work or not work.

Mira carried her full complement of digital devices with her—a fifteen-inch MacBook Pro, an eleven-inch iPad Pro, and an iPhone 12—so work, social media, and entertainment were a keystroke away. After visiting hours were over at the VA, she had hours of free time and plenty of oxy and fentanyl to fuel her introversion and keep her focused while she cruised on her devices. Mira was a research hound, and she loved losing herself and her time wandering down Google rabbit holes. So, on one rainy Portland evening, while sitting in her Airbnb, Mira thought about losing her father and how little she knew about where she came from. She decided she'd ask her father to tell her stories when she saw him next, but, in the meantime, she had time to research her mother's side of the family. She shot off a quick text to Gina, expecting no reply:

I never asked you, and Grandma Rose never talked about her family or where she came from. I didn't see any pictures of her family in her house, except for her husband and her mother, Miriam. Just wondering-what was Nona's maiden name?

The reply came back almost immediately:
It was Blumberg. Rose Blumberg.
Mira asked:
Do you know what her husband's name was?
Again she received a prompt reply:
It was Barak; Barak Del Vecchio. Why are you asking?

Just curious.

Gina continued without prompting:

When Nona was alive, she was tight-lipped about the two of them. I didn't want to bring it up because I figured it made her feel bad. But, after she died, I found their marriage license and marriage certificate from Saint Augustine's Catholic Church in New York. She had them packed away in a trunk up in the attic of her house. I'll take pictures and text them to you if you like.

When you have a chance. No rush.

Gina sent the pictures a few minutes later with a puzzling addition:

Nona shared little about her childhood. I felt like she was hiding something. She told me she was born in New York, and, as a small child, there was a horrible pile-up on the Pennsylvania Turnpike that killed her parents. She told the story that her grandparents and the rest of her family lived in Europe, so she lived with friends of the family after the accident. She wanted to continue in the school where she started and didn't want to live in a country she'd never known. She met my dad and fell in love with him her senior year. He was also from a big Italian family in New York.

She told me they met after he came back from serving in the army in Korea, and that's why he was older than her. You saw that picture of him in his Army uniform that she kept on her end table, right? The entire story seemed weird, and part of me never believed her, but I never questioned her. I wondered why I never met anyone from his family if it was so big and local. I mean, they would've been my grandparents and aunts and uncles, right? I felt like I couldn't bring it up or ask questions. We

*can talk about it more when you get back if you like. I
hope that helps.*

Something ate at Mira. She opened up the files
Gina sent and zoomed in on the picture of the marriage license. June 1, 1960, in the City of New York,
State of New York appeared in the information fields
at the top of the form in a carefully handwritten
script. It listed the bride as Rose Blumberg, with a
birthdate of January 2, 1939, living in New York City.
The form listed the groom as Barak Del Vecchio, with
a birthdate of September 10, 1931, living in New York
City. Mira shifted her attention to the Marriage Certificate from Saint Augustine's Church; the wedding date
stated June 21, 1960.

Playing the online dating game required users
to become adept investigators, and Mira was good at
it. First, she asked Google the day of the week for June
21, 1960, and it came up as a Wednesday. Who gets
married on a Wednesday when they're just twenty
years old? It must've happened in the priest's office.
Mira smelled a secret. She texted her mom back.

To make sure, what's your date of birth?

*December 19, 1964. Mom got me an official copy
of my birth certificate when I was sixteen, so I could get
my driver's license.*

You were her only child?

Yes, that's what she told me.

So she was about 25 when she had you, right?

*I believe so. What's going on . . . Why all the ques-
tions?*

Just curious . . .

K. But I can tell you're up to something.

Mira needed to close so she could get back to work:

It's getting late. I'll be back in touch later.

Mira's stomach fluttered in a way she hadn't felt before. Back on the Internet and following a hunch, Mira searched birth certificates in New York for 1959 and 1960. When she searched under the keywords Del Vecchio, three records appeared on the screen. One stated that Antonio Del Vecchio was born to Rose and Barak Del Vecchio on November 9, 1960, less than five months after their wedding. In addition, the record showed a cross-reference to a death certificate for Antonio Del Vecchio that cited his death on February 6, 1961. He lived less than three months, perhaps from illness or sudden infant death.

The information staring back at her from her computer screen stunned Mira. Gina had an older brother she'd never been told about who'd been born and lost. Plus, Nona Rose was pregnant on her wedding day. She'd kept all this secret from Gina, and now Mira knew the secret. It was as if Mira stood at the edge of a deep crevasse and could easily fall in. She wondered what other secrets she might dig up from the cemetery of her ancestors' history.

Since she was already in the New York Department of Vital Statistics, she looked up Grandma Rose's and Grandpa Barak's birth certificates. Nothing came up for either of them. Why not? Maybe they were born in another state. So she went to the US National Database of Vital Statistics, and while there were other

Rose Blumbergs and one or two Barak Del Vecchios, none matched with their other details.

If Rose was a woman of secrets, could she have been born in another country? Mira opened up the National Archives Database and started a search for Rose Blumberg. The National Archives kept records of all immigrants entering the United States through legal means. She knew Rose's birthdate from the New York marriage license Gina had sent her, so narrowing the search would be simple. Fortunately, she didn't understand how simple. Only one immigration record popped up for a Rose Blumberg with a birthdate of January 2, 1939. It cross-referenced her as the dependent child of Miriam Blumberg, who entered the United States on May 19, 1942. When Mira opened up Miriam's Blumberg's immigration record, it listed her daughter as Rose Blumberg, born January 2, 1939, both of whom entered the United States on May 19, 1942. The immigration papers listed Miriam's birthdate as October 23, 1916, and disclosed that Miriam and Rose were born in Cologne, Germany.

Cologne Germany . . .

In addition, the papers listed their religion as Jewish.

Jewish?
Jewish?
Jewish.

Mira sucked in lungfuls of air. She looked at the screen of her iPhone. It was 1:47 a.m. Her text notification dinged. It was Gina:

Are you still up?

Mira responded:

Why?

I can't sleep. Why are you up?

I'm doing a little research . . . for work.

You got me thinking about Mom and Dad. And Martin. How's he doing?

He's dying, Mom. How do you think he's doing?

Mira regretted her snappish tone and was glad Gina couldn't hear her crunching a fentanyl tab between her teeth. She felt guilty for saying something so mean, especially given what she'd just found out.

I'm sorry, Mira. This is hard on me. I never stopped loving him. I wish we could have spent our lives together. I wish we could have raised you together. I wish we could have had more children together. But we were both children ourselves, and I thought I was doing the right thing supporting his career in the military. And I thought I was doing right by you both by keeping his secret for him. Now I know it was the biggest mistake I ever made.

Damn. Now Mira felt even worse and just wanted to hug her mother. She typed:

I've got to go to bed, Mom . . . get some sleep.

Neither of them was ready to deal with the secret she'd just uncovered. But before she tried to go to sleep herself, she made one last stop on her journey through the immigration archives. She reopened her National Archives browser to look for Barak.

Search keywords: Barak Del Vecchio, date of birth September 10, 1931.

Perhaps five seconds later, there he was: Barak Del Vecchio, date of birth September 10, 1931. Date of immigration: May 19, 1942; place of birth: Rome, Italy; Religion: Jewish.

Jewish?

Jewish.

Mira's head felt as if it would explode. A tsunami of emotion broke over her, and, like a tsunami, it sucked every micron of energy out of her as it retreated. Images of Cossacks storming into villages setting homes on fire came to her. They chased down and murdered the men, threw the women to the ground, and raped them in front of their children. She saw families caged like animals in shacks behind barbed wire, starving, skin pulled tight around ribs with no flesh. Then came scenes of open graves filled with corpses fresh from the gas chambers.

Mira shook with confusion. Terror enveloped her. Ancient ghosts of bigotry and genocide bled from her unconscious. Hopeless grief gripped her soul. Her cells vibrated an unknown and intolerable horror. Then, finally, she tumbled into an abyss of despair, like lifeless bodies tumbling into shallow graves.

Were the drugs overwhelming her nervous system? Was she gripped by a disabling delusion? Was she slipping into the throes of mental illness? And then, just like the tsunami escaping back to the sea, the illusions returned to the collective of her unconscious.

Mira sat silently in front of the frozen computer screen for a few minutes. She sensed deep in her soul that she was about to begin a journey from which she might not return. But she didn't know if she had it in her.

She created a new file folder on her desktop named Family Secrets and saved file copies of all the documents she'd found. She'd share them with Gina when she returned to Seattle and had some time to digest it all. When she closed the folder, she looked at the screen on her iPhone: 3:14 a.m. She fell into bed without taking off her clothes. Two fentanyl brought her into a deep and troubled sleep. From there, she fell into a heavy trance and rejoined the constellation of her ancestors.

| 13 |

"Juden! Raus! Zeigen Sie sich! Wir sind für Sie gekommen. Sie müssen mit uns kommen. Du kannst dich nicht länger vor uns ver.stecken," the soldiers screamed.

Ruben Blumberg and his parents held their breath until the pounding at the front door stopped. The Nazis had come for them two or three times a week for several months, and they had smashed through the front door days ago. Ruben left it broken to appear as if the family had abandoned the house for good. Each time the Nazis came back to check, he, his wife, and his parents huddled like church mice in the basement of his roomy Cologne home. They hid behind a fake wall Ruben had built into the coal cellar. He'd engineered a safe room by piling a veneer of coal against a false facade that he'd built, so it looked as if coal filled the room to the top. Behind the wall was a compact area with a table and chairs, oil lamps, and four cots. He's fitted a secret trap door to the back of the house that allowed the family to enter and exit from their lair, as well as a way for friendly neighbors to smuggle food and other necessities to them. They used the woods behind the house as a toilet and cleaned themselves using the backyard hand pump in the dark of night.

Here's how it came to be:

November 9, 1938:

Ruben tried his best to put out the fire raging in his print shop in the merchant district of Cologne, Germany. A Nazi Youth group had smashed through the shop's front window and torched it while Ruben's father printed invitations for an upcoming wedding on the printing presses in the backroom. Ruben was working on the company books in the business office. Broken glass had cascaded into the shop and rained down on Ruben as he worked, followed by firebombs that drove Ruben and his father out the back door of the shop. While the fire department looked on and did nothing, the Blumbergs stood in the alleyway and watched the business his father started forty years earlier burn out to the building's brick shell.

One hundred German Jews died that day they called Kristallnacht—for all the broken glass left in the streets in its aftermath. In the following weeks, the Nazis rounded up hundreds of Jew.ish men and jailed them. Ruben's family lived in fear for the next months as they tried to decide what to do. His parents argued he should take his wife and get out of the country while they stayed and tried to protect their property and other assets. Ruben argued that they should all stay together and wait it out. He felt that a revolutionary uprising to defeat Hitler would come about to end the insanity, so they stayed, and Ruben started building his safe room. Ruben's wife, Miriam, was seven months pregnant.

January 2, 1939:

While Miriam and Ruben's mother hid in the safe room, Ruben and his father heard the women scream, "Ruben! Send for Sarah, the midwife! Miriam's in labor! This baby is coming now!"

Rose Blumberg entered the world two hours later.

May 1939:

Germany was fighting on multiple fronts all over Europe and winning. Forty percent of the Jews in Cologne had left, fleeing to safer ground. The Blumberg family tried to live a "normal" life even though Miriam knew that darkness was falling over Europe. Death surrounded them and would soon envelop them. So they ventured out during the day, avoiding the Nazis who patrolled the street and brought home a few provisions to sustain themselves along with newspapers to keep informed.

September 1939:

The war entered Cologne proper. Ruben, his family, and all the Jews of Cologne observed the all-night curfew. The quality and quantity of their food rations slipped below that of the general population. They could not use public transportation. Miriam and Reuben's discussions of leaving intensified, but they were worried about being caught on the run. Trying to escape didn't seem any safer than staying.

"Ruben, I'm scared to death staying here with the baby," Miriam said. "The Gestapo stops us every day, and we can't take the bus to town. They're rationing our food, and they treat us like prisoners. We're living like caged animals, hiding in the basement of our own home. This is no life for our new baby Rose. Take us to America. Please. I heard we can go through France. It's the safe way. Please . . . Please." She pleaded with him.

Ruben tried to reassure her. "I can't leave my parents here, Liebe. They'll never leave. Maybe this will all be over soon. They say the Allied forces will come and liberate us. The world cannot leave us all here to die." Miriam already knew otherwise, and by May 1940, Allied bombers devastated large sections of the city daily.

As the situation deteriorated further and the Nazis gathered up Jews around Germany to live in ghetto areas, Ruben finally sent Miriam and Rose to Catholic friends in France. At the same time, he and his parents waited out the war living behind the coal facade in the basement. He made travel arrangements with his good friend Hans to smuggle Miriam and Rose out of the country. Han's family was Catholic and so not suspect. They would stay with his friends in France until everything was safe again in Germany. When they boarded the train to leave, Ruben's wife, Miriam Blumberg, was just twenty-three years young, with her new baby Rose in her arms, just eight months old.

Two weeks later, while Ruben and his parents were reading in their safe room, the familiar sound of hobnail infantry boots pounded onto the floor above them.

"*Juden! Herauskommen! Du kannst nicht verst-*

ecken. Raus!"

A few minutes later, as they cowered in the corner holding their breath, the three of them watched in horror as a bayonet pierced the carefully constructed wall Ruben had built to contain the facade of coal on the other side. Within minutes, the SS demolished their hiding place, dragged the three of them to the front yard of the house, knelt them to their knees in front of their neighbors, and shot them in the back of their heads as if they were rabid dogs.

~

Dearest Miriam,

With the heaviest heart, I must tell you of the death of your husband Ruben and his parents, Hermann and Rifka. Your neighbors informed me the Nazis discovered them hiding in their basement and executed everyone on the spot. We do not know why the soldiers treated them in such a violent way. It was as if they resented your family successfully building such an ingenious hideout and surviving for as long as they did. I am here in France also, so let me know if there is anything I can do to help you. We pray for your family every night.

With our deepest regrets, Frederick Krauss

The news shocked and devastated Miriam, but she had premonitions of the outcome, and she remained stoic for Rose. Also expecting the worst, Ruben had given her plenty of money to start over if needed. She kept it hidden away in the lining of her suitcase. Over the next two years, she and Rose made their way from France to Sweden and finally found ship passage from Sweden to America. While American immigration authorities turned away many Jewish refugees on suspicion of being Nazi sympathizers, Miriam and Ruth gained entry as true Jewish refugees.

~

Meanwhile, in a small flat in Rome, Italy:

"*Pazza pazza, ti ucciderò! Non ce la faccio più. Sei fottutamente pazzo!* You crazy bitch, I will kill you! I can't handle it anymore. You're fucking crazy," Barak's father screamed at his mother. After that, Barak heard the same words at least once or twice per week, followed by the sound of fists striking flesh.

Barak knew his mother was crazy, but she couldn't help it, and he loved her as any son would. She saw people who weren't there, heard voices talking to her that no one else heard, cried uncontrollably one minute, followed by cackling laughter at untold humor the next. But his father's screaming at her and beating her did not make her sane; it just bloodied her face. Barak knew he would kill him one day or die at his hand trying if he stayed. That would not help his mother. So, on this day, he packed his duffle bag with as many clothes and personal goods as he could and made his way down to the ship's docks at the Rome seaport to find his future.

Benito Mussolini was running things in Italy, and the Jews were not in favor there. Barak's family was Jewish, but it made no difference to him as an only child unfazed by politics and anti-Semitism. Moreover, the Allies had not yet entered the war and had not taken over shipping for the wartime efforts. Barak sought adventure and fortune, so he stowed away on the first Italian freighter he saw bound for New York. He wanted to build things and heard that America was all about building things.

How Miriam, Rose, and Barak ended up in the same line on the same day at the same time being processed at the Ellis Island Immigration Center is a mystery. Or perhaps it was what Jews knew as Beshert —preordained. Some say Beshert means finding one's soulmate, and perhaps that's what it was for Rose and Barak that day, even though Rose was only three years old and Barak only ten.

Miriam sat with Rose on her lap, and Barak sat across from her, filling out immigration papers at the large oak table. A German translator sat helping Miriam, and an Italian translator sat helping Barak. When they asked about her and Rose's religion, Miriam said, out loud in English, "Jewish."

Barak knew that word and made eye contact with her. Then, when Barak's translator asked him the same question, Barak looked straight into Miriam's eyes and, also in English, said, "Jewish."

Miriam's translator asked her if they were together, and looking straight back at Barak, she replied, "Yes."

When her husband's Italian Catholic friends came to pick up Miriam and Rose to take them home, Miriam didn't leave Barak behind. Between Miriam's broken English and their friends' Italian, the three started their new life in America together.

Miriam asked their friends to help them become conversos, Jewish immigrants who posed as Christians for safety reasons. They took on the facade of Roman Catholics but secretly kept their Jewish identity. The practice started during the persecution of Spanish Jews during the 14th and 15th centuries and resumed with German immigrants. Miriam learned that White supremacists, the KKK, and other fascists groups openly held anti-Semitic events in the United States. She wanted no part of being identified as Jewish since they didn't trust any government to protect them. Miriam knew she would always be a Jew in her heart, while Barak was only ten and didn't care about any of it.

Miriam would figure out what to do with Rose when she grew older.

The three of them ended up staying a few extra weeks with the sponsoring family practicing their English, and when Miriam used the money her husband sent with her to rent a small flat in Brooklyn, she invited Barak to live with them. She found a decent job in a department store, arranged preschool for Rose, and enrolled Barak in a public school.

Barak lived with Miriam and Rose for five years. He became Rose's big brother, and she, his little sister. But as they grew up together, so too grew an unexplainable connection between them. It seemed as if they'd been together many times before and would be together many times again. While they may become separated again by space and time, they would never be apart. *Beshert.*

Barak had a special talent for designing and building things. So at sixteen, he got a job working on the Brooklyn–Battery Tunnel being built under the mouth of the East River connecting Brooklyn and Manhattan. He loved the concepts of digging tunnels under things and building bridges over things. He moved out into his own flat but stayed close by and spent time with Miriam and Rose.

The US Army drafted Barak in 1950 at the start of the Korean War, along with over a million other men and over another million volunteers. In Korea, 54,000 young US soldiers died, and over 7,500 remained unaccounted for. Barak's engineering and construction skills led him into the Corps of Engineers, keeping him out of combat, and he survived the war. He stayed in the army five years after the war ended before returning to New York and back to living with Miriam and Rose. Only now, Rose was nineteen, with curly ginger hair and gorgeous features. Barak was twenty-eight, dark and Italian.

Beshert prevailed, and they fell into deep romantic love and married. Barak knew of his Jewish heritage, but he honored his promise of secrecy to Miriam. Rose believed herself to be Catholic, so she and Barak married at St Augustine Catholic Church in New York City.

Miriam had another secret she kept at the wedding. She suffered from untreated breast cancer and worried that it would put their lives in danger if the truth came out about her condition. Within six months, she would be dead. So finally, Miriam called her daughter to her deathbed to tell her the story Barak already knew but held secret.

She began, "Rose, I'm so sorry I kept this secret from you for so long. You and I left Germany when you were just a few months old and fled to France because we are Jewish. Your father sent us there hoping to survive the Nazi occupation with his parents so he could bring us home again. But the Nazis discovered your father's hiding place with his parents soon after we left and murdered all of them and took our belongings. So you and I continued to America just two years later. We met Barak at the immigration center. He was just ten years old and came from Italy. He was Jewish also but mainly needed to leave his family. So we took on the religion of our Catholic friends who took us in so we all could remain safe."

Barak chimed in, "I checked on my family a year after I came to America and learned they all died in Auschwitz after Germany occupied Italy in 1943. If I'd stayed, they would have killed me, too."

Rose remained silent as she listened to Miriam and Barak's stories. She felt a confused and deep sadness, but a memory began stirring inside. Finally, she spoke: "I remember you braided loaves of bread and baked them for Friday night dinner when we stayed in France. When you finished with the bread, you braided my hair. You thought I was too young to remember, but I do. We sat at the table, and you covered your eyes and lit the two candles every week. Then you said the same prayers over the wine and bread each time. I believed you didn't want me to talk about it, that it made you too sad. But I remember . . . I remember." They all cried quietly together for their ancestors.

Rose and Barak held Miriam in their arms as she took her last breath. They bathed her body and sat with it for twenty-four hours before they buried her in the Jewish tradition. The Orthodox Jews of New York who helped bury the conversos in the Jewish tradition quietly arranged a traditional funeral for Miriam so no one would ever know.

Within the next five years, Rose and Barak moved to San Francisco, so Barak could help build the Transbay Tube under San Francisco Bay. They honored Miriam's wishes and kept her secret about her family being Jewish and dying at the hands of the Nazis. Gina was born and baptized in the Catholic Church and never knew the truth. The family treasured two years of joy and love together. But, on a tragic day in their third year, Rose received word that Barak had died in a freak construction accident. Barak's death devastated Rose and left Gina fatherless. With Miriam and Barak gone, Rose remained an orphan and a widow destined to live her life alone. She never remarried. She grieved for Barak every Sunday in the Catholic church she'd joined for Gina, and also every Saturday morning as she secretly recited the Kaddish, the Jewish prayer for the dead, standing straight and tall beside her bed.

| 14 |

The morning following her vision, Mira awoke clutching the small cross she wore around her neck. It had hung there since her Catholic confirmation at age eight. The artifact meant little to her, other than the habit of wearing it. She wore it as a symbol of her belonging to her mother's and grandmother's community. Now the touch of it confused her.

She had learned little about the Holocaust in Europe and the extermination of the Jewish people there at the hands of the Nazis. No public school teacher had spoken of it in her study of history, and no family member had spoken about it when she was growing up. She knew one or two Jewish children in school but felt she should avoid them. She knew that Jewish people didn't celebrate her holidays and had holidays of their own, but she didn't know what they were or what they meant.

She also knew nothing of the history of the devastation of the Jewish people at the hands of the Catholic Church in Europe, beginning in the twelfth century and continuing for hundreds of years. During that time, the Church had set up the Holy Office of Inquisition to root out and punish what they called "heresy," even though those religions predated Catholicism by centuries. Those not claiming to be Catholic had to leave their homes, submit to conversion to Catholicism, or face execution. She also didn't know about the pogroms of Russia, where the governing party segregated the Jewish population, raped the women, murdered families, and burned their homes to the ground. The persecution of the Jewish people throughout the millennia had never been a part of her education.

Mira relaxed a bit when she thought about Miriam, Rose, and Barak escaping to America. Beshert was unknown to her, but she had heard about kismet —destiny—and believed it. She closed her eyes and saw Miriam sitting at the table in the immigration building with Rose on her lap and Barak sitting across from her by chance, filling out their immigration papers together. She saw the German interpreter helping Miriam and Rose and the Italian interpreter helping Barak, the three of them having never met before.

Mira imagined the love story that would take place in secret over the years that followed. It would be a story kept secret from her and her mother Gina; a story of fear, and love, and ultimate tragedy, never fully disclosed save for the scraps appearing on Mira's computer screen in the records of the National Archives of the United States of America. Miriam, Rose, and Barak had all passed on, and their secrets passed with them–secrets perhaps lost for all time save for Mira's curiosity and research skills.

And deep in the shadows of her unknowing,

what was Mira to believe about herself based on her discoveries? Her great grandmother and grandmother, their husbands and brothers, their sisters and cousins, nieces and nephews were all Jews. Had they all perished at the hands of the Nazis? Had any survived?

Had any others made their way to America and hidden their true identity? Did some still live in secrecy in Germany, or perhaps in other countries around the world?

Clearly, Rose had named Mira in honor of her mother, Miriam. Since Miriam and Nona Rose were Jewish, wasn't she? Wasn't Gina? She touched the cross around her neck, wondering if she should take it off. Who was she, really? She found the confusion overwhelming. Anxiety and exhaustion wracked her body.

Her father lay dying just down the street at the Veteran's Administration Hospital. He had perhaps only days to live. Mira sat with him for hours every day of the final three weeks of his life. She decided not to share her discoveries about Gina's lineage with him during his last days on the planet. Perhaps he would share a bit of his own history with her before he left. She was more interested in reconnecting with him, taking care of him, and loving him. She would deal with the secrets of Rose's family later.

So she read to him, fed him, and wiped his face with cool washcloths. She dozed in an easy chair while he napped. Each day, his breathing became more labored. She knew she was watching him fade away, but she felt only peace and love for him. Then one night, as she slept in the chair across the room from him, she heard him call out to her in the same powerful voice she'd heard the day he taught her to ride her bicycle:

"Mira, come here and listen to me."

"What, Dad? What is it? I'm right here."

"I know things about you. They come to me at night during Dreamtime. I know drugs have you within their power; we share that weakness. I became addicted to drugs, trying to recover physically and emotionally from my wounds. Without knowing it, you became addicted while trying to connect with me. You were reaching out to me across the divide that separated us. Perhaps you aren't ready to accept it yet, but you're an addict. You want to believe you can control your drug use, but you can't. Our shared trauma, our shared history, and our shared addiction bonds us to each other.

"Maybe you think you're young, and you're just playing, and you'll deal with it later. But you're playing with death. You think it's no big deal, but it's bigger than big; it's bigger than you, and it's bigger than me. You think you're managing it, but it's managing you. You think you're smarter, but it's outsmarting you. Underneath it all, you're lonely and think badly about yourself. I've spent the last thirty years feeling lonely and thinking badly about myself. You connect to me in my addiction, and I connect to you in your addiction.

"After I move to the next realm, find your own strength in yourself and recover from your addiction, or it will kill you as it has killed me. Try to discover what gets in your way. Learn what I didn't learn: to love yourself completely to the depth of your heart and soul. Find your true purpose in life, not just what brings you the recognition of others and financial rewards. Live your life to the fullest. Find real and lasting love and discover your true nature and calling. It is our true purpose for being that we must find during our lives."

Martin's words burrowed into Mira's soul. They infused into her and transformed her. His message was undeniable.

~

Mira's eyes fluttered open. She rubbed the sleep out of them, and the room came into focus. She still sat in her hospital chair while her father dozed quietly in the bed across from her.

Mira walked to her father, bent over, and gently whispered words to him that came from outside of her, "It's okay to let go, Dad. You don't have to worry about Mom or me any longer. We'll be okay. I'll always remember you. I'll never leave you or forget that you're with me. I'll look after Mom, and I know you'll look after both of us from beyond. I'll see you in the cherry blos.soms along Lake Washington that bloom in the spring, and I'll see you in the ducks that tend to their broods in the summer. You'll be with me in the mist that covers the waters of Lake Washington in the fall and the flames of my fireplace in the winter. I'll carry your name with me throughout my days and look for you to greet me when it's my time to join you. I love you." Mira kissed her father gently on his forehead and silently left his room. She knew that her father needed to be alone to complete his journey.

When Mira returned to her Airbnb that evening, she gave her mother a call to let her know what she'd found out about their family history. She paced around her room as she worried about how Gina might react, but she hoped they could begin a discussion about what she'd learned. She'd always felt her mother hid things from her, so she hoped she'd at least be open to listening to what Mira had found out in the records. Gina answered Mira's call on the first ring.

"Hi, honey. I'm glad you called," Gina said in a staccato voice.

Mira hated her mother's trite terms of endearment, but she ignored it. "Hey, Mom, I found out some things I want to talk over with you. Do you have time to talk?"

"Always for you, hon . . ."

God save me, Mira thought.

"You said Nona Rose told you she was born in New York?"

"Yes."

"What would you say if I told you she was born in Germany . . . Cologne, Germany?"

"That's impossible," her mother replied. "She had no accent."

"Well, I just found out that Nona was born in 1939 in Cologne, and her mother brought her to New York in 1942. So she grew up in New York, but she was born in Germany, and they emigrated to the US in 1942. So that's probably why she had no German accent."

Gina said nothing.

"Mom? Did you hear me?"

"So her entire family came to the United States?"

"No, it looks like just her and her mother."

"How do you know this?" Gina asked.

"It's in the records the government keeps."

"The government?" Gina said with an edge. A staunch conservative Republican, Gina voted along party lines no matter what.

"Yeah, Mom. They've been keeping immigration records on file since the early nineteenth century. That's where I found Nona Rose and her mother, Miriam. The records listed no one else from her family, so I cross-referenced the immigration records with a ship's passenger arrival record from the same date, and there's a match. And the really crazy part is that Nona Rose's future husband, Barak Del Vecchio, arrived on the same date from Italy as a stowaway on an Italian freighter seeking asylum in the United States because of family abuse and religious persecution. He was only ten years old.

"They must have all met at the immigration center, and I think Nona Rose's mom Miriam took Barak under her wing and raised him as her own. It looks like they had a Catholic sponsor family helping them, and Miriam brought family money from Germany. Barak must have grown up with them for a while and then joined the army during the Korean War—we know that part of the story from Nona Rose. What we didn't know is that they knew each other from before and might have all lived together with Miriam as a family of immigrants from Europe."

A long silence stretched out on the other end.

"Mom? Did you hear me?"

"This is bullshit . . . you must've gotten something mixed up with the records of some other people. You want me to believe that Mom was two when she came here from Germany with her mother Miriam, whom I never knew; that my dad, Barak Del Vecchio, who died in a construction accident when I was three, and I remember sitting on his lap and playing with him on the floor, came to this country alone from Italy when he was ten and met my mother and her mother at the immigration center in New York, right?"

"Right."

"And Grandma Miriam and Rose came alone, without Rose's father or any other family, and never went back, right? And that Mom made up the story that a drunk driver killed her parents when she was a kid?"

"It sure looks that way."

"What the hell are you smoking down there in Portland, anyway . . . or did you steal some of your dad's oxys? So answer me this . . . why the hell would just the three of them travel from Germany to the United States in 1942 and never go back and never have the rest of their family come over? It makes no sense."

Mira avoided her mother's sarcasm and forged ahead. "Well, there is one more fact contained on the immigration papers that explains the whole thing. Do you want to know what it is?"

"Sure, it can't get any weirder than this." Gina chuckled nervously.

"Think about it, Mom . . . what was going on in Germany in 1942? Adolph Hitler was sending all the Jews in Germany to the gas chambers. All three of our relatives, Miriam, Rose, and Barak had their religion listed on their immigration papers. Jewish. They probably took on the identity of Catholics when they lived in New York out of fear of being persecuted here. Apparently, lots of Jewish immigrants did that."

Gina responded immediately and loudly. "Now you've really gone off the deep end. We are Catholic. All of us. Nona Rose was Catholic; your Grandpa Barak, me, all born and raised good Catholics and nothing else. Mom and Dad met in high school. They were both raised Catholic and married each other at Saint Augustine's in New York—you saw their marriage certificate. They baptized me and confirmed me in the Catholic Church, and I did the same for you. You must have gotten someone else's records. There have never been Jews in our family. It's impossible!" Gina shouted.

She continued into a full-scale rant, one that Mira had heard before. "Jews always create problems. They murdered our Savior. They are cheats and liars and money grabbers. They deserved what they got in Germany. I'm just sorry Hitler didn't finish the job."

"Mom, stop it. Please, please stop it." Mira sobbed. "I can't take you talking like this. Regardless of whether this is the truth, I can't take you talking like this. It's wrong. No one should talk this way about anyone. My God, Mom, my father, Martin, your husband, the man you claim to have loved, is a person of color. You fell in love with and married an African American man. And I am your child, a child of color. Dad is a descendent of slave families, stolen from their homes in Africa and brought here illegally. Right now he's dying here in a hospital bed just down the street, and you're hating on your own people. I can't handle this." Mira sobbed. "I can't handle this . . . he'll die any time now."

The connection went dead. Gina had hung up and cut her off mid-sentence. Predictable.

Still crying, Mira crunched a fentanyl and let it dissolve on her tongue. When she started to relax, she opened her laptop and clicked the folder on her desktop called Family Secrets. She started rereading the contents. Her reading and the opioids brought her the blessed sleep she longed for, sitting there in the comfortable recliner of her Airbnb. Her computer slid unharmed onto the carpet. As she slept, a vivid dream of her ancestors' journey came to her once again, but this time in a variant and confusing form.

~

A handsome man drops his young wife and small child off at the home of his good friend Hans. She carries one small suitcase containing two changes of clothes inside. Sewn into the lining of the suitcase is a large sum of cash. When the young father and mother kiss each other goodbye, and he kisses his small baby on her forehead, he mutters, "Auf wiedersehen; until we meet again."

She pleads with her husband to come along, fearing she'll never see him again. But instead, he reassures her that her fears are without merit. That the danger will soon pass, that he will send for her, and they will be together again back in their home in Cologne when all the political turmoil in Germany is over.

Hans supplies the woman and her child with fresh identification papers, along with train tickets to ensure their journey to France is a safe one. Then, he smuggles them in the dark of night from Cologne to Frankfurt, where they board a train for France. In France, they wait to make their way by ship to America.

About two years later, a young Italian boy, only ten years old, sneaks aboard a freighter bound for New York. He has had enough of his father's beatings and his mother's insanity. He's grown up too fast in the chaos of his family. When he lands in New York, he sits at a table across from a young mother holding a small child on her lap. They know they've been together before and will be together again. They haven't heard the word yet, but it's Beshert.

But in this lucid iteration of Mira's vision, everyone she sees wears the blue-and-white-striped, pajama-like uniform of the prisoners caged in the concentration camps. The inside of everyone's wrists shows a distinct six-digit blue tattoo, the same ID number that's sewn onto the breast label of their uniform. The family she leaves behind, Hans, the train personnel, the friends in France, the passengers and crew on the ship, the Americans who greet them in New York, the immigration workers at Ellis Island, and even the Nazis who patrol the streets of Cologne and murder her family; yes, everyone living on the planet, in every country on earth, they all wear the same blue-and-white striped uniforms and bear the same tattoos displaying their prisoner number on their left breast. On everyone's right breast, a yellow patch displays a Star of David emblazoned with the name "Jude" on it.

~

Mira awakened in the morning moist with perspiration, her vision a vague disquiet deep in her gut. She looked out the window of her Airbnb at the light streaming in from outside. She needed to get to the hospital, but after last night's call to Gina and the dream that had come in her sleep, she had to pull herself together. She'd been here for almost three weeks now, and she knew the end was near. But she had an important stop to make before seeing her father, and it would take some time to complete.

Mira arrived at her father's room late in the morning with some fresh flowers to brighten his room. When she opened the door and peeked inside, the nurse quietly removed the IV tube from his wrist and the oxygen tube from his nose. His eyes were closed in the most peaceful way she'd ever seen. He had passed, not wanting to upset her with the last goodbye.

Mira had said everything she needed to say already, and a sense of peace enveloped her, like the embrace of loving angels.

When the nurse finished, she said to Mira, "Take as long as you need. I'll be back later."

Breathing gently, Mira sat, holding her father's frail hand softly in hers. Through her tears, she looked down at the freshly applied ink drawn that morning on the inside of her wrist. It simply bore his name, Martin. She sat with him for over an hour, saying her last farewells, softly stroking his hand, and quietly humming songs she didn't know. A collection of her tears lay on the floor below. Finally, when she could sit no more, and her tears had gone, she rose and slowly left the room. As she moved through the door, an emerald-green ball of light departed from the center of her chest and floated to the far corner of the ceil.ing, where it joined with the emerald-green ball of light of her father before it departed into the cosmos.

| 15 |

Mira felt numb during the train ride back to Seattle. The gray Northwest drizzle outside the window filtered the beauty of the landscape into dark silhouettes. Most of the seats were empty save for a few napping business commuters. The fentanyl coursing through Mira's veins no longer salved the gaping hole in her heart opened from the loss of her father. It no longer quelled the rage festering in her soul for her mother's secret.

Why did you keep this secret from me? You cheated me out of all these years of connection to my father. Why did you decide for me, decisions that were mine and mine alone to make? She gazed hypnotically at the healing tattoo on her inner wrist—Martin.

You had no right! she screamed to herself. Drugged cells held her physical fury silent while her mental rant raged on: You should have told me the truth from the start. You could have forbidden him from going on that deployment. You could have done that. He'd already served his country enough times and had a wife and child on the way. I had no say in the matter. And, when they shattered his body, he needed to come back home so we could care for him—

our home, our care. You could have taken him to treatment, weaned him off the drugs, found other ways to relieve his pain. Our love could have made the difference. Instead, you let him suffer alone with no one to love him or for him to love. Our love would have made the difference. Instead, you forgot about him and what that would do to me and brought that monster Russian who hurt us into our house.

The sudden thought of Sergei dislodged a remote body memory from Mira's drugged unconscious. The gag reflex in her throat went unnoticed before it vanished again into the depths of her shadow memory. Mira's jaws ached from clenching the rage she felt with her mother inside of her. It seemed impossible for her to fill the hole in her heart.

When she arrived in Seattle, she left the train, picked up her bags, and crunched another half fentanyl on the way out of the Amtrak station. Six weeks had passed since she'd left for Whistler. Ian had left on tour while she'd been with her father. She tried to remember what he looked like and the feel of him inside of her. The memory of Ian had faded, like the pictures of Martin's parents her father had given her the day before he passed. She needed Ian now more than ever and knew she could entice him home between gigs with one sexy nude text.

However, vague dizziness and nausea came over her as she slipped out of the Uber outside her condo. As usual, Mira's key card passed her through the front door, elevator, and condo door, requiring no fishing in her bag. But the symptoms doubled with each threshold she crossed. Finally, she stepped into her condo, paused for a moment just inside the front door, and tried to catch her breath and calm her stomach before she rolled into the bedroom.

Mira stopped in Ian's room. It seemed empty. She opened his closet and drawers and found them bare. His guitars and electronics had disappeared from the living room, as well. She knew he never took all his equipment on gigs. If not for the white, sealed envelope bearing her name neatly printed on the front leaning on the fireplace mantle, she would've thought he'd been a delusion.

Perhaps she'd entered a scene from a crappy movie or a pulp novel. She pulled another half fentanyl out of her purse and crunched the bitter pill between her teeth. The caustic dose burned Mira's tongue as she tore open the envelope. She sat with the folded single sheet of paper for what seemed like days, and then she finally took a breath to read contents she could already guess.

Dear, dear, Mira.

Two dears? What the fuck is that supposed to mean?

I might as well just come out and say it. I met someone while you were recovering. At first, I thought it was just sex . . .

Yeah, that makes me feel better.

. . . but it turned into something bigger.

Knowing you, probably bigger tits.

Long story short, she's come with me on the road, and she inspires me.

Probably it's her tongue that inspires you, you dumb asshole.

I'm sorry I left in such a crappy way, but it is what it is.

Such intelligent language!

I wish you all the luck in the world. Sorry about your dad.

Oh, he remembered.

Ian.

It often worked, but this time Mira's sarcastic anger didn't dent the lead sheath of her desolation. Anger had always been her go-to feeling at her lowest moments, especially with men. Whenever her girlfriends complained to her about their boyfriends, she delivered her patented response: "I mean, they're all assholes at the core, aren't they?"

Rage fueled her to get her through anything. She called it "righteous anger." Righteous anger meant warranted resentment, justified outrage. Indignation that anyone would feel if it happened to them—fury demanded by the gods. She'd always mustered rage to propel her forward.

But not today. Her devastating physical trauma, followed by her mother's lie about her father's death and cover-up about his existence, followed by sitting with him through his last days and finally losing him again, brought her to her knees. Ian's desertion was the coup de grâce, the death blow.

The anger disappeared as quickly as it had come, replaced by a raw terror that erupted from her gut. Her recent discoveries from searching the immigration records came back to mind amid the devastation of losing her father and Ian. What had happened to Nona Rose and Miriam's family in Europe? Who were her ancestors, and were any left? What was her true identity? Could she believe anything about herself? Was everything about her and her family a lie?

With tears cascading down her cheeks and dripping from her chin, Mira cried out for a shred of hope from her childhood days with her treasured Nona. "Nona, why couldn't you tell me the truth? Where are you? I need you now!"

In desperation for something real to hold on to, she cried out, "Okay, Google, play Louis Armstrong's, It's a Wonderful World."

Louie's soulful voice began warbling around her:

I see skies of blue and clouds of white . . .

Mira slumped deeper into her ivory leather recliner. She scanned her stark room from wall to wall, realizing she'd never called it home. She referred to it as her "place" or her "condo." She looked at the slate-gray walls, devoid of art and bare of photos of friends and family. In a trance, she dug into her purse, pulled out the prescription bottle of fentanyl, and dropped it on its side on the end table next to her. She reached over, picked it up, and deftly popped off the cap with one hand to fish out a single tablet with the other.

Pulverized by her teeth, the harsh chemical numbed her tongue and her mind. Her breathing slowed as the hole in her heart expanded. She no longer heard Louie's words as they lost their meaning in her despondency:

The bright blessed day, the dark sacred night . . .

Mira's senses dulled further, and her eyelids fluttered closed. She descended into a state that was unfamiliar but strangely recognizable. Mira's brain no longer controlled her muscles, and her rational mind no longer managed her decisions. Raising the capless bottle of fentanyl to her lips, she threw back her head, emptying the entire contents into her open mouth, choking all the remaining pills down her throat and into her stomach.

The deadly overdose moved through the walls of Mira's stomach and into her bloodstream. The synthetic chemical made its way to the opioid receptors of her brain. What began as an attempt to obliterate her pain turned fatal to her living organism. All parts of her sank into desperate, dark oblivion. Numbing darkness enveloped her.

Mira's fixed eyes could not blink. Her chest rose and fell imperceptibly as her heart slowed with each breath. Her body, brain, and emotions slowly died as her spirit separated from her body. Her descent into oblivion brought no expected comfort and resulted in no relief. The darkness brought no clarity, no resolution. The gloom created no amnesia and the blackness no ending. A void entrapped her. Her breathing slowed to nothingness as a single final thought passed through her dying mind: Was this my true purpose in life?

A final shallow breath entered Mira's lungs, only to remain unbreathed.

All was still . . . all was still.

All but for the sound of a distant, imperceptible voice.

| 16 |

Mira's spirit separated from her body, then merged with and moved through the ceiling above her. She gazed down upon the lifeless, narcotic-infused body she'd once occupied, and which now lay below her. Not yet free of her human-mind experience, confusion filled her.

"I hate that body. It's skinny, and her chest is too small. But I'm free of it now, so why do I care? Just let me get through this ceiling and be on my way. God! Will I ever be free of this incessant thinking?"

God . . . ?

Her therapist had nagged her about practicing daily meditation to calm her anxiety-ridden mind. During sessions, she'd droned on and on about mindfulness and living consciously "in the moment." It never made sense to Mira.

"Let me get this straight," Mira said. "You want me to sit in a chair for twenty minutes twice a day, thinking about nothing? That's bullshit!"

Her therapist's facial expression had remained blank, and she'd said nothing in response. Mira never admitted that she believed she possessed a fatal flaw that no one could ever repair during those sessions.

She decided meditation was way too lightweight for someone so fucked-up, and she finally stopped going to see her. Her therapist never asked Mira about her drug use, and Mira never offered to tell her.

"Jesus! Why am I thinking about my fucking therapy sessions? Why am I not moving on?"

Jesus?

A tiny flash of light interrupted Mira's all-too-familiar internal dialogue of random and unnecessary thoughts. It looked like one of the shooting stars Mira had witnessed in the deep night sky out by the creek behind her house when she was little. The tiny glint streaked up into Mira's unfettered consciousness as she looked down on that fragile body. She focused on the source of the light. It came from a single unfallen tear, glistening in the corner of the lifeless eye, staring up from below. Transfixed by the glint, Mira encountered a soft voice of pure energy from beyond.

"Liebe, the tear speaks to you. You must listen."

"What?"

Confused, Mira asked, "Who are you, and what do you want?"

"The tear, Mira . . . it invites you on a journey."

"Who are you?" she demanded.

"Who I am is not important. If you must, think of me as a guide or perhaps a companion. I promise I will not lead you astray. The tear; it has a message for you. Let it show you."

In that instant, Mira merged with the tear. She became the tear. And, in that merging, she became her grief. Exquisite, searing heartache enveloped her and burned through the hard.ened shell of her embodied life all the way to the core of her spirit.

"Get me the fuck out of here!" declared her dying human brain. "Just get me the fuck out of here now!"

| 17 |

Rather than an escape from reality, Mira found herself returned to her fourteen-year-old body.

~

The physical shock to Mira's private parts was violent and unexpected. The drugs and alcohol in her bloodstream dulled her consciousness, so only her cells imprinted the physical pain as body memory, along with terror and shame. Visual and mental memory dropped away immediately. However, nothing protected her from the accompanying injury to her soul.

Her friend Mel had been having sex with her boyfriend for months and promoted it to Mira as the best thing ever. What neither knew was that Mira's body had become contaminated long ago with the ghost of a dark and terrifying energy buried in the crevasses of her psyche. Her cells remembered, but her mind had blissfully forgotten. Now, in this new state Mira had entered, she was a fully conscious observer. As the guest of the uninvited guide who'd joined her, she was inside her fourteen-year-old body and assessing the experience at the same time.

Weird.

House parties during the week were a regular part of high school life. Most of the kids in her class came from single-parent homes or two-income parents, both off to work from 8:00 a.m. to 5:00 p.m. five days per week. For Mira, latchkey living had become the norm from early on, and so had daytime unchaperoned house parties when she attended high school.

Most house parties took place at the homes of the senior boys. Students left school at lunchtime, not to return for the rest of the day. Parents left their supplies of alcohol and prescription medication stashed in their liquor and medicine cabinets within easy reach of their children, while other students raided the cabinets in their own homes to add to the supply at the party house.

Unknown to Mira and the other underclass girls at the high school, the junior and senior boys had a secret club. They called it the Sophomore Club. The upper-class boys competed to have sex with as many of the freshman and sophomore girls as possible. They met together secretly before the parties to plan their strategies. They became adept at supplying just the right combination of alcohol and drugs to the girls to make them compliant and powerless to resist. Their parents' Valium and Xanax paired with beer and whiskey worked great on demur fourteen-and fifteen-year-old girls. Scoring a virgin counted double.

Mira had never had sex before and didn't understand that she was worth extra points in the boys' game. She knew kids were having sex at the house parties and thought that, at some point, she might have her first sexual encounter at one. She was standing off to the side of the living room when an older boy approached her carrying a full bottle of amber liquid. He was tall, clean-cut, and handsome—a boy she thought her mother would approve of.

"Hi, I'm Chris," he proclaimed to Mira. "I haven't seen you before. Are you new here?"

"This is my first year at high school; I'm a freshman from Lincoln Junior High."

"Wow, I went to Lincoln but graduated three years ago. How is the old place?"

He was great at drawing Mira out and helping her relax. He invited her out onto the back deck, bringing along two plastic cups. He put the cups on top of the deck rail and poured about an inch of whiskey into each one.

"Have you had whiskey before?"

"Sure," Mira lied. "My mom lets me drink at home."

Mira downed the drink in one swallow, turning her head to hide the fire running from her throat to her stomach. Chris immediately poured a fresh glass for Mira while he sipped from his. After a few more rounds, he placed two small, white pills down next to Mira's glass. They were full-strength Xanax tablets from the robust stash his mother believed she'd successfully hidden under the panties in her dresser's top drawer. Benzos and alcohol, a perfect blend to induce a combination of anesthesia and amnesia, especially for a nubile neophyte. She popped the pills obediently and washed them down with the whiskey.

Oblivious to the blackout that engulfed her, Mira regained a shred of consciousness sometime later in a room she didn't recall entering. Her mind fought to identify where she was, and her mouth fought for a bit of moisture. Finally, she determined that she lay flat on her back. Glancing to the left, she saw an empty bottle of whiskey on what appeared to be a bedroom dresser with a mirror attached. The image of a naked male thrusting downward reflected in the mirror. Her gaze transfixed on the image of his bare bottom, rising and falling as if watching one of the porn movies her stepfather had stashed in the living room of their house.

As she slowly returned to consciousness, Mira realized that her shoes, pants, and underpants were no longer on her body. She realized that she was the girl underneath the boy in the mirror. Still heavily sedated by the alcohol and the benzos, she couldn't call out or resist. She continued to gaze at the scene in the mirror, paralyzed in her body and unaware of her spirit, looking down from above.

With her consciousness returning further, young Mira knew the body on top of her was without emotion or care. His groans and pants were without love or compassion, just the sounds of animal release. When younger, Mira learned about touching herself. She discovered on her own that her natural juices flowed easily and freely when she gently pushed one or two fingers inside until her body released in exquisite pleasure. This boy pushed big and hard inside her without patience or concern. Her body was closed and dry, making the physical pain excruciating. He pushed harder and faster without awareness of her experience, conscious only of fulfilling his physical destiny.

Now fully aware of what was happening to her and not wanting to be present for what was going on, Mira's fourteen-year-old spirit moved quietly to the ceiling. Separated from her body, she watched from above with clinical curiosity as the boy violated her body and her fragile psyche below. Then, a hazy transient memory of other male and female body parts moving together flitted through her consciousness, followed by the image of a tiny creature floating lifelessly in a pool of water. As she watched the girl on the bed below being raped, she wondered why she clutched at her throat, gagging and choking, unable to breathe.

She stayed on the ceiling while the boy got up from the bed and took time to clean himself. He acted as if Mira's scent disgusted him. As he left the room without a word, Mira slowly re.turned to her inebriated body, now further contaminated by the energies and fluids he'd placed inside her. She didn't remember his name, and he never asked hers.

As she got up from the bed and straightened her clothing and hair, some small part of her appreciated the boy's unfettered lust for her. A piece of her felt the power of possessing something he didn't possess—a power that fulfilled his need. And another part of her felt the animal pleasure in her cells stimulated by the unabated sex, yet she simultaneously felt betrayed by those same cells.

And then, in a nanosecond, a tsunami of shame obliterated the entire experience and sent it deep into the oblivion of Mira's unconscious. Once safely tucked away, the shame morphed into a torrent of self-loathing about herself; she was worthless, wrong, dirty, and guilty. Before leaving that room, shards of bright-orange light fell like shattered glass from Mira's aura and scattered around her feet as her spirit shed tears of grief and longing. Then, the wave of shame turned back and retreated into the deepest recesses of her memory. It etched upon her soul indelible words that looped incessantly through her unconscious: I am worthless. I am dirty. I am broken. I am unlovable.

~

"Why have you brought me here?" Mira asked her companion. "Why must I remember this? What purpose does it serve? Just let me finish dying and find my peace."

"Peace does not come in death, Mira. It comes with consciousness and healing."

"Fuck consciousness and healing! Memory brings torment, pain, and grief."

"Have patience, Liebe; have patience. They say the devil is in the details. So before you complete your transition, let's look at more details you might not remember, or were not aware of, about the life you just left."

"Have at it if you must. The sooner I 'complete my transition,' the better."

| 18 |

"I hate you; I hate you; I hate you; I hate you; I hate you."

Mira imposed the task on herself like one of Mira's grade-school teachers assigning her to write one hundred times as a punishment for unacceptable behavior. With each repetition written in neat rows in her art book, her anger and frustration with her mother grew. By age eight, Mira called her mother "Gina" to her face, knowing that it cut her. Her father had gone off to war, never to return. Nevertheless, Gina had always told Mira that her father loved her deeply and had given his life in service to his country.

Service to his country? I don't even know what that means, much less what war's all about, Mira thought to herself every time her mother brought it up.

"Sometimes countries don't get along and fight with each other," she'd told her, as if a few simple sentences painted a prettier picture in contrast to the stark horror that was the truth of war. "They send soldiers who fight and kill each other. Your father was a soldier and died for our country."

Mira got into fights at daycare, but no one died.

So why did her father die?

Gina showed Mira color pictures of her army ranger dad in full camouflage fatigues. Dressed from top to bottom in body armor, battle helmet, and dark glasses, he looked like something straight out of a movie. The image of her father scared and confused her all the more. She had no conscious memory of him, and the pictures Gina showed her completely obscured his facial features, including his dark chocolate skin. To her, it could have been a picture of anyone.

Mira's heart ached to know her father. She'd given up asking Gina her unanswered questions:

"Why did he leave us? Didn't he love us? Why was fighting a war more important than staying home with you and me? If I died, would I be with him again?"

Over time, the ache in Mira's heart grew into desolate emptiness. Finally, it became so unbearable that she no longer consciously acknowledged it. Instead, she buried it in a hidden place where her longing morphed into craving, first for food and sugar, and later for alcohol and drugs.

Gina had turned to alcohol and men long before she met Martin and before she lost him to war. Rose had church friends, one of whom had an older son who molested Gina when she was less than six years old. He told her it was a special thing that friends did, and they must keep it a secret from their parents. If she told her mom what was going on, it would really upset her.

It happened whenever they came to visit. One

night during dinner, Gina stuck a fork in his thigh under the table as he crept his hand between her thighs. Rose and her friends were busy talking and didn't hear the boy's muted yelp. Gina smiled a bit while she pushed the fork a little deeper as she continued picking up one pea after another from her plate and putting each one in her mouth. He never touched her again, and neither ever spoke about it further. But, by then, the sexual abuse she'd endured had planted the seed of addiction. Gina started having full intercourse with boys when she was thirteen and never looked back.

After she married Martin and birthed Mira, her addiction to men continued to flourish. She cheated while Martin was away on deployments, rationalizing that he mustn't care or he would've stayed at home. She developed a simple system of feeding her compulsion for sex: using coworkers at her workplace during the day. The sex was zipless. She would steal quickies in a bathroom stall up against the wall or in a seldom-used supplies closet bent over a counter. Sometimes, she set a goal before she got to work. She notched one or two encounters per week. Orgasms didn't matter to Gina, and she rarely experienced them. Attraction and emotion played no role in her compulsion. Married or single, fat or thin, tall or short, it didn't matter. She was not interested in finding a new partner. She remained completely in love with Martin and missed him painfully. The power she exerted over the mindless men who lined up to cheat on their wives and girlfriends intoxicated her. Risk and secrecy were potent drugs that drove her need.

It shocked Gina when, on her last visit to Walter Reed, Martin made it clear they needed to say goodbye forever. Even though every cell in her body said no, she agreed he was right, that she and Mira needed to move forward in their lives without him. She sensed Martin's shattered spirit and, without thinking, buried her doubt in the decision he'd made. She held her tears until she left his room, then sobbed torrents in her rental car parked outside. Secrecy came naturally to Gina, so she pulled herself together, returned home to Mira, and easily maintained the story she and Martin had created.

For the first few months, Gina committed herself to live the life of a single parent until she finished raising Mira. After all, she'd been a happily married woman. Her friends promoted the idea that she should wait a reasonable amount of time, start dating again, and then find someone new to settle down with. Knowing her own nature, Gina knew her role as a mother would become adulterated if she focused on landing another man. But her resolve proved short-lived.

Gina's relationship with Sergei started innocently enough. He owned the small construction company Gina had hired to take care of the rotting porch that faced the creek behind their house. Martin had reassured her he would rebuild it on his next leave home. Now that he was never coming home, Gina needed help with the project, and she had financial resources from the spousal disability checks that arrived every month.

Sergei's parents had immigrated to the United States from Russia during World War II. They'd seen enough of a brutal war up close and personal and had no intention of bringing their children up in the instability of the Russian government. After emigrating, they settled in Boston and opened a successful dry-cleaning business, allowing Sergei to grow up with relative stability and good fortune. The family only spoke Russian in the house, and he struggled with the shame he felt when he heard his parents' thick Russian accent out in public. Otherwise, he enjoyed a life of ease, spoiled by his parents' abundant good fortune.

Gina's friend Margie had used Sergei for some construction work around their house, so when a stair on the porch collapsed under Gina's slight weight, Margie sent Sergei right over. Gina hadn't been with a man for many months and was unaware of the moistness she felt as she spoke with him on the back porch. She hired him on the spot, and he came back the next day to begin work. He spent the first day tearing out the old wood and piling it into his pickup truck to haul away to the dump. Then, early the next day, he returned to put in new deck piers and floor joists. Gina brought lemonade out to him later that afternoon, and they sat for a few moments on one of the new beams.

When she got up to take the pitcher and glasses back into the kitchen, Sergei pulled her down toward him and kissed her deeply. When she didn't resist, he stood up and pulled her into the shed at the back of the yard without saying a word. She melted into him, grabbing his crotch on the way. Once inside, he boosted her onto the workbench and, in one swift motion, lifted her dress to her waist and pulled her soaked panties to one side. She unbuckled his belt, popped the snap of his Carhartt work pants to let them fall to his ankles, then guided his sizable manhood inside her with her hand. They were both oblivious to the small, still form watching quietly from the shadows just outside the door.

Sergei moved into the house within the week and never left. He was ten years older than Gina and showered her and Mira with gifts and attention. He had a contagious laugh and an outrageous sense of humor. Like many tradespeople, he walked through the front door every day at about 4:00 p.m. carrying his requisite six-pack of beer. Mira noticed the slight shift in Sergei's energy by beer number four, and, by beer six, she felt downright nervous around him. The smell of cigarettes laced his beer breath, and, as the evening wore on, his face moved closer when he leaned over to speak to Mira while they sat on the couch watching TV.

Mira wished she had a lock on her bedroom door but didn't mention it to Gina. She was already afraid of monsters under her bed and sometimes screamed out in the middle of the night. Gina would sleepily come into Mira's room and reassure her that monsters didn't exist and that her imagination played tricks on her. But Mira remained inconsolable, knowing that a monster had already made its way into their house and was sleeping in her mother's bed.

"Get me the fuck out of here now! Something's wrong!" Mira screamed.

"What is it, Liebe?"

"I don't want to be here! I don't want to know this! Why won't you let me die? I just want to die! That's all I want . . . I don't want to know this."

"I know, Liebe, I know . . . but we must."

| 19 |

"You're horrible," Mira told her companion. "You've brought me to the gates of hell. What have I done that's so wrong to deserve this? You're torturing me. If this is what I must do, then send me back. I've made a mistake. Send me back . . . I beg you . . . send me back!"

"Please, Liebe, you can do this. It would be best if you did. Please! I am here."

~

A dream, perhaps? A nightmare for sure. First, an alien odor. Asleep? Awake? The scent grows stronger, acrid. Now an acid taste. Overpowering brackishness and stink. Disgust now. Asleep? Awake? Dream? Real? Imagined? Mouth pushed open—disgusting smell and taste. Eyes squeezed shut. Don't look at the monster— you don't want to see. Mouth pushed open further, pushing down inside. This snake monster is killing me. I can't breathe. I'm dying.

I can't talk—can't scream.

Snake Monster trying to go down my throat. Gagging, choking, disgusting odor, awful taste, pushing further, faster, harder. So little . . . Open my eyes? See the monster? Awake? Asleep?

Dream? Mom says no monsters. But I know the monster is here. The monster is real.

She takes a look—sees the contorted face of the monster, eyes squeezed shut, pushing. Suddenly, the monster's eyes fly wide. Fiery red-orange disconnected eyeballs. Terror. Too much to bear. A familiar face, glowing red eyes. Sergei's eyes. Terror. Won't survive.

Her inexperienced eyes close, her spirit disconnects, her mind misunderstands. To survive, she must move this event deep into her unknowing mind. She leaves her body and moves to the ceiling, unaware of the presence of the visitors who have joined her. They see and recognize the shattered shards of orange-yellow light falling from the little one. Fragments of her soul fall and scatter onto the floor of her bedroom.

~

"Liebe, she believed she endured this horrible episode all alone. Her mother and father were not there to protect her. But she was not alone. We were with her throughout. We, along with the other angels."

If Mira still had her heart, it would've exploded out of her chest. "Not alone! What the fuck are you talking about? We were there along with her other angels? Then why didn't we all stop him?

"Look around, you idiot. She's alone. Her mother's asleep in the other room, and her father is dead, but not actually dead. He's not there to protect her. Not alone? What the fuck do you know, anyway? You're a hallucination of my dying human mind. I'm hoping I'll finish dying soon, and you'll stop torment-ing me."

"I understand your anger and frustration, Liebe. You misunderstood. You thought you would be able to leave straight away. I wish it were that simple. We can take a break from this part for now. We will revisit under different circumstances. Perhaps if you witness your beginning in this lifetime, you'll have a better understanding of this and other events that have brought you here."

"Whatever," Mira snapped.

| 20 |

At nineteen, Gina's body knew while her mind slept. Snuggled in the wall of her womb, a few tiny cells divided themselves. Yet, aside from the indiscernible fatigue and nausea, all seemed normal. No one ever explained that she had a cervix.

Less than four months earlier, a handsome young man wrapped in the crisp uniform of the United States Army drove the short thirty-five miles from Fort Lewis Army base south of Tacoma to spend a weekend partying with his buddies. These horny male soldiers liked the Seattle scene for their short leaves—lots of places to find hormonal young women looking for a little excitement to break up their mundane lives. Soldiers provided unexpected fun without attachment. The girls called them "tags," and the soldiers knew them as "tag chasers."

A good place for underage girls to troll for tags was the Pike Place Market just up from the waterfront. The soldiers shopped there for inexpensive gifts with local flavor to send home to their family members or the hometown girlfriend waiting for them. Local girls hung out in the myriad of coffee shops around the market, waiting for a tag to notice them. One of Gina's favorite hangouts was RealFine Expresso overlooking the bay.

When three tags strolled through the shop's front door, Gina casually looked up from her friends and her latte. Of the three, one face mesmerized her. Onyx light exploded from his rounded features, illuminating everyone around him. Had he been female, she would've called him beautiful. So when he and his friends asked to share the community table they occupied in the crowded shop, she was afraid he could hear the buzzing of her cells. Gina tried her best to keep the flush from her face and the quiver from her voice as they exchanged stilted conversation.

The two of them finally found an excuse to split off from their cohorts to spend the rest of the day together foraging the fruit and craft stands in the market, and, when he presented her with the small bouquet of Skagit Valley tulips he'd slipped off to buy while she wasn't looking, she was his. They found a room that night that Martin could afford at a quaint bed-and-breakfast on First Avenue just around the corner. They spent the entire night together, waking up and having breakfast downstairs. Their love-making was nervous and halting, innocent and pure. Neither had ever spent a full night in a bed-and-breakfast with a lover.

They became inseparable for a few months before he shipped out. He regularly came to Seattle on leave, and she traveled to Olympia to stay in a cheap motel near his army base when he had to work on weekends. Finally, he left on a secret deployment without giving Gina details about his mission. Instead, he gave her a special PO box where she could contact him while he was away, not knowing if he would respond, or even if he would return.

A few weeks after he left, Gina started feeling nauseous and tired. When she missed her period, her friends convinced her to have a pregnancy test. Once she confirmed she was pregnant, she considered sending him a letter about the surprise she carried inside of her from their time together. But she felt sure she'd never hear from him again, and she'd abort the baby.

Abortion was not alien to Gina. Her mother Rose was an old-school Catholic who checked her daughter's menstrual periods each month. It was her form of a pregnancy test. After Gina missed two periods when she was fourteen, her mother dragged her off to a private abortion clinic. Her second abortion came at sixteen, and that time she took care of it herself. Now she was nineteen, and while she didn't want to have another abortion and felt they were wrong, she didn't want to raise a child as a single parent.

Mira witnessed Gina's struggle as a young woman and cried out from beyond, "She planned to abort me . . . she didn't even want me!"

"Liebe, that's what you concluded back then in her moment of indecision. Your spirit was hanging out, waiting to occupy those first few cells dividing inside of Gina. What other belief could you form without thought, without experience, without consciousness."

"I couldn't have known what she was feeling—I wasn't a person yet. How could I have known she didn't want me?"

"It's quite a mystery how you knew, isn't it, Liebe? We really don't know everything about how the universe works. Yet now you know that some part of you knew her feelings then, anyway. She was going through quite a struggle, wasn't she?"

Confused, Mira turned her attention back to Gina's story.

At first, finding out she was pregnant devastated Gina. She wasn't ready to have a child, and she didn't want to burden Martin. Distraught and overwhelmed, she felt guilt and shame for being so impulsive and not protecting herself better. But this pregnancy felt different. Her relationship with Martin felt real to her. He was her mate. And the being swimming inside her seemed to communicate her presence and her desires. So when Gina considered aborting her, she experienced grief she'd never felt before.

She wrote to Martin and told him the truth. His quick response was exciting and terrifying:

I love you and want you to live with me and be my wife. I want us to be a family. So marry me and have our child. It would devastate me if you did otherwise.

Martin married Gina on his next leave home. They bought the tiny house in Maple Valley with the creek out back before he returned to Afghanistan. Gina, Martin, and Mira lived the family life for the next six years of his military career while keeping his deployments on special ops a secret. Gina felt angry when Martin re-upped for another four years without discussing it with her, but she knew he loved his work and the excitement it provided. He intended to fulfill his commitment to active duty and then try to take himself out of harm's way by becoming a training officer for special operations soldiers.

While he was on active duty, Gina operated a daycare at the house. It allowed her to take care of Mira before sending her off to kindergarten when she was five. She planned to return to community college to become a medical assistant when Mira started school and Martin returned from active duty.

Martin came home on leave just a few weeks before Mira's sixth birthday. He taught her how to ride her bike on that leave, and the two of them formed a deep connection that seemed impossible to break. Martin left six weeks later, telling Gina and Mira that he'd be home for good soon. The shattering call about Martin's devastating injuries came on Mira's sixth birthday. Gina couldn't stop crying. Martin had been forty-five days away from coming home to stay.

Gina dropped Mira off to stay with Nona before flying directly to Landstuhl Hospital in Germany. She stared blankly at the seatback in front of her for the entire flight. She didn't understand that her life would never be the same. Then, outside the closed door of Martin's hospital room, a nurse and doctor talked to her in low tones, trying to explain to her what she was about to witness. When she walked into the room, she was glad Martin didn't see her slip to her knees or hear her sobbing as she knelt beside his bed, gripping his limp hand.

Martin lay in a medically induced coma with tubes attached to almost every organ left in his body. Gina was thankful that the carnage the fifty-caliber round wrecked on Martin's body wasn't visible under the bandages and blankets that covered him. The brilliant light reflected from his jet-black skin had gone out. He awoke a few days later, and they removed his breathing tube. Gina and Martin spoke quietly to each other, discussing issues and making frank and realistic decisions. Five days later, Gina left his room, leaving her tears and her anger behind. They would part company forever and tell Mira that Martin had died of his combat wounds.

"I don't understand," Mira said to her spirit companion. "Why must I see this? I lost my father when I was six. Then I lost him a second time a few weeks ago. They both kept it a secret from me. Why weren't my feelings considered? How does it help me to know this now?"

"Be patient, Liebe. It helps to know the nature of your beginning at the time of your ending."

"That makes no sense."

"Let's go back even further. Time works differently than the way they told you it does. Imagine for a moment that we experience many endings and beginnings, not just this one. And, if you imagine you've experienced other beginnings before the ending you're experiencing now, and will experience more beginnings to come after this ending, try to take a moment to be present to the specific circumstances of this beginning . . . your beginning in this unique life. You must experience the truth of the beginning of this lifetime and learn about its meaning for your future lifetimes."

"Are you crazy? You're blowing my mind! What the hell are you talking about?" "Instead of trying to explain it to you, let me show you your last beginning now."

~

If Mira had a stomach, the sudden drop would have turned it upside down as if she was barreling through the vertical loop of the roller coaster at Six Flags in California. But having no vocal cords with which to scream, her unembodied terror remained trapped inside. She existed only as random electrons merging to create new life, as universal forces—energies not yet in embodied form—attracted and organized chaos into substance, turning un-embodiment into embodiment and quantum physics into abstract human emotion.

The descent, a visceral dropping and tumbling down-ward—even though dropping, tumbling, and downward didn't exist—continued as a fall into embodiment, absent of distance and duration, concepts only of human making. A clump of cells growing in fleshy folds of an organism patiently waited for a confused spirit, eager to begin anew but devastated by disunion from the divine. Wisps from other beginnings and endings contaminated its purity. As spirit and cells merged, the grief of separation settled in. Predictable conclusions formed in the new spirit—

concepts without language, emotions without rationale—"I am separate, exiled, cast out. I must navigate this new form alone, disconnected. This state of being is unsafe and dangerous. I alone must find my way; there's no one to protect and guide me."

Without challenge, these damning concepts formed the core operating system for this existence. This beginning followed by the recent ending was inevitable. These beliefs, formed in the chaos of organizing, became the foundation of all that followed. If left unchanged, they would silently govern every decision made.

~

With the download complete, Mira's spirit paused and quieted. "I always felt so alone. Perhaps if I had understood..."

"We are innocent at the beginning, Liebe, become informed in the during, and can integrate at the ending. We come to understand by becoming conscious through the experiences of each lifetime and the core beliefs those experiences create." Mira's developing consciousness widened a bit. Then, after a moment of reflection, she asked, "How do you know all this?"

"Oh, Liebe..." he replied, "... you taught me all this at the time of my ending."

| 21 |

Compressions on her chest and another person's breath in her lungs sucked Mira back into her limp body for an instant. The emptiness in her heart and the disabling fear in her gut remained. Her human lungs burned and hurt. Finally, her eyelids parted just enough for her gaze to fall on the name-tag pinned to the chest of the charcoal-skinned medic leaning over her. "Marty," it said. He squeezed the breathing bag in his hands like a fireplace bellows, but the embers of Mira's life remained dark and cold. Her body failed to sustain its own heartbeat and breath, and her eyes closed again, returning her to oblivion.

"I'm pushing another cc of naloxone into her thigh. Keep CPR going until the Narcan takes effect. She's hardly here. We'll only intubate if the Narcan doesn't get her breathing again."

~

"Liebe! Come back! We're not complete . . . we have more to discover," the far-off voice called to her. "Come with me to one of your very first beginnings—one that is important for you to know about."

Mira returned from her body. "If it's the only way for me to finish dying, let's go."

~

A young forest girl paused her riverside walk and leaned over a grassy bank to take a long drink of the clear, cool water flowing beside her.

"You want me to believe that's me?" Mira asked. "Not likely."

"Perhaps . . . or perhaps it's just an interesting story," her friend replied.

For the first time, Mira noticed he spoke with a slight accent.

The forest girl gazed into her shimmering reflection: boney brow ridge, bold and prominent; naked skin—pale and covered with long, fine, ginger-colored hair; small breasts tipped with light-pink nipples, high and taut. The image in the water pleased her. She'd lived thirteen summers now.

"Why have you brought me here? And why are you showing me this?" Mira asked. "I'm not interested in some primate girl living in the forest long ago. Let me finish dying and move on."

"Be patient, Liebe. There's no past or future here, just now. Please, try to experience her experience."

The rich forestland provided the forest girl's tribe with everything they needed; berries and edible plants, along with long beans—fresh, clear water to drink flowed in the springs and creeks. The tribe provided for all her safety needs; the tribe was her family. Once she grew beyond suckling at her mother's breast, everyone in the tribe cared for her and each other—mothers, fathers, grandparents, uncles, aunts, cousins, all unnamed. Other strange family roles and customs would arrive 200 to 300 millennia later as societies became more complex, chaotic, and dysfunctional. Control and influence would replace care and concern.

The forest girl's tribe moved about to find additional sources of food and shelter, especially during the dark and cold times. As she grew more mobile, they expected her to keep up and help carry. When she grew tired and could no longer keep up, any of the males or females who noticed swiftly picked her up and perched her on their hip or back. Once she could keep up on her own, she learned about foraging by tagging along with anyone handy. After she'd pushed her from her breast, the female who birthed her no longer paid close attention to her. By the time her hair thickened under her arms and between her legs, she'd finished learning to forage for herself.

Her forbearers had discovered fire several hundred thousand years earlier before leaving the warm areas of Africa to move to the colder climes of Eurasia. They built fires at night for the tribe to gather around for warmth and to cook their food. The entire tribe enjoyed the warmth of the fires they kept burning at the mouth of the caves her people occupied, and they learned to cook their plants and meats.

Recently, the forest girl had noticed a bump forming inside her stomach. She'd seen how the other females' bodies formed bumps—then rounded before they squatted and dropped their little ones. But she was unaware that her body was going through the same change, that a little one grew inside of her. Her primary drives were to find food during the light of day and some safe-haven during the dark; nothing else mattered.

But today, by the river, the movements and rumblings in her belly that steadily rolled through her grew stronger. Sometimes she'd thrown up her food, and a big rolling pain came from deep in her gut. Over time, the movements grew more frequent and intense. As the movements grew, so did her fear and concern, but both subsided when she slid into the warm water of the pools she'd found.

One day while she relaxed in the hot springs, waves of pain began that built into an endless barrage of earthquakes exploding inside her. A brief pause followed each peak, only to return with greater furor. She'd seen this happen with the other females as they went off to drop their little ones. With each explosion, anger charged into her like a wild boar. Fear roiled in her like a cauldron of white-hot magma, subsiding, then erupting again with a vengeance she'd never experienced.

Mira could hardly contain herself. "This is ridiculous . . . we shouldn't be watching this. She needs her privacy. This is no one else's business. I want to look away."

"But, Liebe, it's the beginning of life . . . someone must bear witness to our beginning, just as someone must bear witness to our ending."

The forest girl, her legs splayed to the sides, peered down into the heated fluid surrounding her naked female body and witnessed a small head, not unlike her own, emerging from be.low. He emerged with cheeks swollen and eyes squeezed shut, his face contorted and covered with a thick layer of ooze.

The forest girl knew she differed from the males of the tribe, with their flat muscular chests and strange protuberances between their legs. They sometimes appeared from behind while she drank from the river and forced themselves into her. She became accustomed to that. But no one prepared her for this. She felt as if she was being split in two. She knew something had been growing inside her, and now she realized this was her time of pushing out a little one, like the other females of her tribe.

But she wasn't ready and had no interest in caring for a little one. Livid with anger and disgust, she grunted and moaned and screamed out in pain as she pushed this object, this thing, this being out from inside her, out from the opening between her legs.

She had no memory of being dropped onto the forest floor by the female that had birthed her when she'd first arrived here. But that female knew what to do; she'd suckled and protected her.

The males who'd mounted her not so long ago didn't know or care that she was an innocent girl or that this would happen to her. They mounted her without regard, pushed into her without care or concern, and finished thrusting into her with grunts and shrieks. When they withdrew from her, they left and went their own way. For her, it was new and mysterious and felt good after the pain. This was the way of the forest people, her people. But she had never seen or experienced this part. She felt angry and hurt and scared, and she didn't know what to do. So when this slimy object slithered out of her body and dropped into the water, she left it there and ran away into the forest. She'd had enough of all this. She ran from the pool, leaving emerald-green shards of light from pieces of her soul dropping into the water along with the tiny, lifeless body floating there.

The memory of her experience in the hot springs that day faded quickly. She was happy to have it over with. When she grew older, she mated with one male. Her male left the cave each day and returned as it grew dark to bring food back for her and the little ones. He enjoyed mounting her, and she liked it when he did. The first time, when she'd been younger, that male had forced her with no regard. She hadn't known what he was doing and hadn't been able to stop him. Now she knew and knew her male would stay with her.

She bore more little ones, like the one that came out of her body that day in the hot springs. With each new birth, the fleeting memory of that day came to her. And, with each new little one, she felt a strange feeling she'd never felt before. Other little ones and old ones had died since, so now she knew of death and knew that the little one she'd left that day had died in the water. She couldn't bear returning to the hot springs to relax. Secretly, she thought of the little one every day. She felt a deep sadness about her not knowing back then; she'd just been so angry and afraid.

When she thought about that day now, she noticed another feeling inside her. Perhaps others had felt it also, but they had no way to communicate this feeling, no way of telling if others of her tribe shared such feelings. Such a powerful feeling . . . one that could destroy her or help her learn. When one has done something that hurts another, the feeling comes when one violates a trust or covenant. It's a feeling without a name yet, yet she felt bad, wrong, flawed, and worthless.

"Liebe, do you feel the shame she feels?"

Mira remained mute.

The forest girl reached the end of her life; her body was dying. She'd lived many summers past the time when she'd birthed her child in the hot springs and left him to die. She'd completed her life's purpose, birthing the young of her tribe and caring for the old ones, and she was ready to move on. As she breathed her last breath, she felt no fear. She'd developed no concept of moving from her realm to another, no thoughts of what came before or what would come after. All is just as it is.

When the forest girl breathed her last breath and joined the Light of the Mystery, the feeling with no name lay heavily upon her. With no release, she carried it with her into the beyond, bequeathing it to all the spirits that would come after.

~

"Why do I see this?" Mira asked her spirit companion. "This has nothing to do with me. Her life makes me so sad. This is exactly the pain I wanted to leave behind."

"Liebe, if her life and death have nothing to do with you, why would it make you sad?"

"Because no one protected her and prepared her for what was coming. She was alone and unaware, an innocent young girl with no power of her own. She had nothing to be ashamed of. She was innocent!"

"Then ask yourself this: how might it be that you know so well how she feels?"

Mira paused for a moment before crying out to the universe, "Oh my God . . . was that me?"

And as suddenly as he'd appeared, he disappeared.

"Wait!" Mira cried, "Where are you? Answer my question! Was that me? I need to know! Please tell me! What am I supposed to do now?"

Nothing.

"Please come back! I need you!"

Nothing still.

~

Marty sat on the floor of Mira's condo next to her lifeless body. He wanted to scream to her, "BREATHE!"

He reported to no one in particular, "She's crying." He hid his own tears from view by leaning over her, waiting for the Narcan to make its final decision.

His assistant continued applying CPR and said, "She's still showing unresponsive."

~

Alone in the cosmos, Mira felt strangely at peace. Like the scent of lilacs that lingers after their season has passed, this state seemed oddly familiar. In this place of nothingness and every-thingness, she'd been here before in this state of simply being as pure energy with the memory of her experience. Longing for peace, she took a millennium to rest.

| 22 |

"Mira, come and join me!" The voice sounded bright and familiar. "I'm over here. Join me!"

"Nona, I see you!"

Nona sat at Mira's favorite table at Realfine Coffee in Pike Street Market. She looked younger than the last time Mira had seen her, lying in her casket at the funeral home. Her eyes were clear and sharp, like winter icicles glistening in the bright afternoon sunlight. "Come have tea and scones with me."

Mira moved toward Nona's table, taking short, careful steps on unsteady legs. She slid her cane in front of her, struggling to keep her balance. Translucent skin covered the back of her hand that gripped the handle of her silver-metal cane, showing dark blue vessels underneath. Light-brown age spots dotted her wrist and forearm. Her knees ached as she made her way to the table and slowly eased into her chair.

Both ladies sported graying ginger hair, one wearing it double braided to each side of her head, while the other wore a thick long single braid hanging down from the center. They wore dresses of a forgotten era, flowered, and old European.

A young woman distracted them as she walked

by their window. She seemed on a mission. The two ladies looked at her in unison, and she looked back. Did they know her? Their expressions invited her to join them, to take a break from her hurried chaos, to have a cup of tea, and sit and talk with them for just a moment.

The young woman's face flushed red, and she appeared panicked. She turned her head to the street as if she imagined that everyone passing by looked directly at her. Her eyes dropped to the sidewalk as she reached out to the wall of the building as if to steady herself. She disappeared as quickly as she had appeared, and both women understood.

Mira turned her attention back to her table and peered into the loving hazel eyes of her grandmother. She felt herself relax. The grand lady sitting across from her glowed with soft golden light. Although her perfectly braided hair had become faded and streaked with silver highlights, her skin remained milky and moist.

"Nona, where are we?"

A sly grin curled at the corner of Nona's mouth as she looked directly into Mira's soul. "Why, my love, we are at your favorite coffee shop having tea and scones together."

Without breaking eye contact, Mira stammered, "No, we're not. And you're not my Nona."

Nona's eyes flashed brighter, and her sly grin widened. "Would you be sitting and visiting with me if I had no familiar form, or if I spoke in a voice unknown to you? I've come to you in the form of your choosing, of your creation."

Mira frowned. "When I was young, they taught me you're the one who creates all that is. Now you tell me I can create you. You're confusing me."

"They make up stories to convince us we have no direct connection to the source of all that is," Nona said. "They want us to believe that we must have an intermediary to link us to the divine realm, that the source is outside us, that we require a church or a temple and a priest or a minister to act as the conduit. Some people become cynical and believe they create such stories to control or take our money away from us, so they abandon all belief or hope in a power greater than themselves. They become fearful and depressed."

Mira's eyes glazed over a bit at Nona's heady discourse, but she remained quiet. Then, Nona's cobalt-blue eyes deepened to a rich royal blue as she continued, "So consider this possibility: what if I am you and you are me? What if we are one-and-the-same at the same time? And, what if we manifest each other in whatever form we want and can transmute that form whenever we wish?"

Nona's eyes flashed deeper into a blazing sapphire blue. "And what if time wasn't linear? What if it were bendable, or circular, or concurrent? Could we live many lives, with many endings and many beginnings? Perhaps some beginnings could be endings, and some endings, beginnings? And what if we live some lives in parallel and live multiple lives at the same time?"

Without her knowing, Mira's mind shifted one degree left.

Nona's eyes softened and returned to their wonderful cobalt-blue color. "All interesting questions, but questions for discussion at another time and another place. We don't want to waste this wonderful moment on rational theories, do we? Would you like more raspberry jam for your scone, dear?"

After taking a bite of scone and a sip of tea, Mira spoke. "All I know is that when I visited with Nona as a child, she told me she had long talks with you. She told me you were always there with her and with me, and I could talk with you whenever I wished."

"Did you believe her?"

"Honestly, I was very young, and I didn't know what she was talking about, but I loved her so much I nodded as if I did," Mira explained. "She talked about you whenever we got together, and when I was older and understood what she was talking about, I wanted to believe her. She was just so sure. So when I was alone and afraid, I tried to find you and talk to you myself, but nothing happened. Then, when I was older, after she'd died, I forgot about you and what she'd said. It was all so confusing. I finally decided I had to figure out life on my own, that there was no one to guide me. Ultimately, I decided I had it all figured out; I decided you didn't exist, or, if you did, you'd abandoned me, and I had to make it on my own."

"Mira, do you remember the last time we were together?" Nona asked.

"Yeah, it was when you were in the hospital

dying of cancer. It devastated me. I didn't know if I could go on without you. I felt like you were abandoning me. And now I know you kept your whole life secret from me. Now I know you were born in Germany and immigrated to the US with your mother Miriam when you were two years old. All you left me with were questions. When I found out you kept so many secrets from me, I was so hurt and disappointed. It was like I couldn't believe anything about you after that.

"I need to know the truth now. Did you and your mother escape the Holocaust? Was your whole family Jewish? Did they all die in the gas chambers? Did you lose your whole family? Am I Jewish? Is Gina Jewish? If you were Jewish and escaped the Nazis, why in the world would you become Catholic and raise Gina and me Catholic?" Mira yelled and cried at the same time.

"Whoa! Whoa! Slow down there, girl! You forget who I am. I'm here as your Nona Rose, but, remember, I'm not your Nona Rose. I understand how you feel, and I might have a way to help you. Now that you've become disembodied, there's a perfect way for you to have all your questions answered directly."

In that instant, the spirit of Mira merged with the spirit of her true grandmother. And, in that merging, Mira was Rose. And, as Rose, Mira knew everything about Rose, and even all about Rose's ancestors. Instantly Mira knew all Rose's secrets and the answers to all her questions. She saw the generations of Jews who came before her and all those who'd perished in the genocide of anti-Semitism. She tasted the richness of the millennia of her culture, and she suffered the pain of their trauma: from their enslavement and torture in Egypt to their exodus to the Promised Land; from their torture and expulsion from Spain to their travels to the New World; from their genocide in Europe to their rebirth in the Land of Israel. And, in an instant, she knew everything she needed to know, even why Miriam kept her true story a secret and raised her daughter Catholic. And Mira felt at peace with it all.

"Let me pour you some more tea so we can get back to my last question," Nona said as she lifted the teapot and poured steaming tea into Mira's cup.

Mira cleared the fog from her spirit, settled back into her chair, and tried to remember Nona's last question. Finally, Mira asked, "What did you ask me before?"

"I asked you if you remembered the last time we were together. I meant when you entered your last inter-life when you were in between your last life and this life."

Mira frowned. "You mean I was here before? We were together before? That makes no sense. I remember nothing like that."

"I understand. Let me try to help you remember. It was just before you decided you wanted to enter a body again; you wanted to finish up some things you hadn't completed the last time. You were so brave, ready to have another go."

"You've got to be kidding me. Finish up some things? Have another go? Are you crazy? I'm still trying to get the hell out of here and never come back. If everyone would quit interrupting me, I'm more than ready to move on now."

Nona paid no attention to Mira's tantrum. "When we were last together, you had an obvious intention, and you were sure you wanted to go back. But you became confused and afraid when you transitioned from formless to form. You decided you'd made a terrible mistake and that you had to do it alone. And, in that moment of terror and confusion, you forgot you were not alone. You forgot I was still with you, and the entire universe was with you and supporting you. So when you took that tumbling descent into that clump of cells growing in the wall of Gina's womb, you were totally disoriented, and you misunderstood. If you like, you can go back there again, but this time knowing I was there with you and that you were safe."

"Go back there again? If I like? Now I know you're a crazy figment of my dying brain. I read an internet article that people experience what's called dying-brain hallucinations at death. That's got to be what's happening now. So why in God's name would I go back to the last time I came into my body? No one in their right mind would choose to do that again."

"Why in God's name?" Nona queried.

"Oh, shit!"

Without pause, Mira returned to that tumultuous fall from there to here. Again, she plummeted from the cosmos into being, changing from pure energy into embodiment. Again, she tumbled head over heels, twisting and falling, upside down and rightside up, like that roller coaster at Six Flags. Again, her stomach flew into her mouth as light and dark kaleidoscoped around her. But this time, for the duration of her long, chaotic, terrifying descent, she knew that a presence traveled with her. Loving energy attended her, creating a safe container for her as she careened into life.

During her dizzying drop, Mira looked beside her, and there on that roller coaster seat next to her sat eight-year-old Nona, her head thrown back, laughing with abandon, arms flung high above her head, screaming and giggling. Tears streamed down her youthful face as she reveled in her ride. Nona's bliss and joy, so total, dissolved all of Mira's fear, and she joined with her newfound partner, throwing her arms above her head, screaming out loud, and laughing with abandon all the way down the exciting ride into life. Finally, they arrived together at their destination, conscious of their connection to the Source of all that is, all that ever was, and all that ever will be.

And suddenly, Mira was an old lady again, sitting with her dear friend Nona, sipping tea and eating scones at RealFine Coffee at Pike Place Market.

And she knew . . . she knew . . .

After a moment, she asked, "Are you God?"

"Oh, Jeez . . . that. That's what some people call us. I really get sick and tired of all the names. Some say there are 10,000 names for the divine. Everyone keeps trying to figure it out. I enjoy calling us 'The Mystery beyond all Mysteries.'"

"Us?"

"Yes. You and me."

"You and me?"

"Yes. You, and me, and everything else. Everything that is."

"I'm confused . . ."

"Exactly! Confusion is essential. You spent your young life trying to make sense of the senseless. You expected to solve the mystery of life instead of living the mystery of life. When you realized no one had a reasonable explanation, and even science had only theories, you tried to explain the unexplainable. In that moment of terror, when you were tumbling into that little clump of cells buried deep in Gina's cervix, you decided it would be less terrifying if you could explain it. So you made up a story. When the story didn't work anymore, you tried other stories. When all the stories didn't work, you gave up, and your life lost its meaning. Ultimately, you gave up on life."

"You're making me fucking crazy with all this theory!" Mira protested. "Maybe you're just making up another story. You sound like a cross between a Sunday school teacher and a philosophy professor. Dammit, show me!"

"There is only one way for me to show you. Are you willing to come back with me and see for yourself?"

| 23 |

"I'm afraid you're pregnant."

The doctor's robotic pronouncement lacked any empathy and fell on Gina like a truckload of rocks. Shock overwhelmed her nervous system throwing her words into a staccato of words over which she had no control.

"No, no, that can't be. It was just a one-night stand. We met at the market. He was beautiful and strong, and I wanted him. I'd met no one like him. He'd barely enough money to get us a room at the Pensione Romero around the corner from the market. We spent the night together looking out over the bay. I've never spent the entire night with a boy before. It was the first time I felt like someone made love to me. He was shy, and gentle, and kind, and wanted to make sure I found him pleasing," she explained, as if credible evidence might somehow grant mercy upon her and reverse the doctor's draconian pronouncement.

His face remained devoid of empathy, so Gina continued her panicked babble unabated:

"Sex was always something I did drunk in the back seat of a car or my bedroom when my parents were out of the house. Sometimes I thought I heard

Mom listening at my door, but she did nothing about it. This was different; it was so nice to wake up together, curled around each other. We got dressed, came downstairs, and drank espresso, and ate croissants. They served us in the dining room, where we sat on matching chairs at an antique table. The owner was so sweet to us. She sat down with us, and drank coffee with us, and talked about Seattle with us. I felt so adult and refined. I've never felt that before. Back then, I thought I was still just a silly kid."

The doctor blinked and shifted in his chair.

"When we left," Gina continued, "we walked down by the waterfront before he had to get back to his base. We exchanged phone numbers and mailing addresses, but I never expected to hear from him again. Instead, he started calling me the next day and called me every day for the next two weeks until he went back on deployment. That was six weeks ago, and he's been writing me every day since. It's been nice, but I haven't known what to do. I wrote back, but I'm not used to this."

Not a flicker of emotion or support came back from the poker-faced doctor. "He sounds special," he said flatly, "but we have to deal with this pregnancy now."

"My period was due two weeks ago, and the home pregnancy test came back positive. So I came in to make sure, but I already knew . . ."

The two of them sat together in silence for a moment.

Gina's eyes bore into the floor in front of her.

"And he is very Black . . . mom will have a cow." Looking up, Gina searched the doctor's face for judgment. Still no flicker.

Longer silence.

"They can arrange an abortion at Planned Parenthood," the doctor finally said. "You're old enough to decide on your own. No one ever has to know."

From their observation perch, Mira and Nona sat in silence, observing the interchange.

Then Nona said, "Your mother wasn't ready for you and was beside herself with fear, guilt, and shame. While you were descending into the clump of cells growing in Gina's body, you soaked up her shock and overwhelm and started reacting to her experience and feelings."

"Reacting? I had no form yet. Fetuses can't react . . . I didn't have a brain to create any feelings or reactions."

"We don't need a developed brain to form concepts and reactions. We record and store feelings and reactions in the structure of our cells. Every human cell has its own individual nucleus that acts as its brain. Each cell in our body 'remembers' feelings and experiences on an energetic level. The nucleus controls all the cell functions the same way our physical brain controls our body. Your cells divided and multiplied as you grew inside Gina, and the two of you shared the same blood supply. You felt Gina's fear and shame as your own, so you created your own conclusions and reactions to cope."

If Mira still had a mind, she'd be trying to wrap

it around all she was hearing. "So even if I bought what you're selling, what am I supposed to do about it now?"

Nona smiled. "Well, you can join in with them again if you like. It's your choice, but this time, with consciousness, understanding, and healing."

Before Nona finished her thought, Mira descended into that clump of cells growing inside Gina. Instantly, she became engulfed in Gina's shame, anxiety, confusion, and isolation. She felt the feelings and perceptions entering and being recorded into her own cells. She was privy to Gina's thoughts and feelings and struggled to keep them separate and differentiated from her own.

Mira heard Gina's thoughts and felt the effects they had on her. "This is awful," Gina muttered to herself. "It's the worst thing that ever happened to me. I'm so ashamed! Mom will kill me. And Martin can never know; he'll think I'm a slut . . . It's all my fault for getting pregnant, and he has his entire life ahead of him."

That night, immersed in desolation and loneliness, deep in her anxiety and grief, Gina sat on the edge of her bed, drinking her mother's vodka and holding a bottle of anxiety pills. Mira floated inside her. Shame and confusion overwhelmed Gina. She took several swigs of vodka and removed the cap from the pill bottle. Tears dripped from her cheeks. Mira struggled to discern her own experience from Gina's. Finally, Gina's sense of desolation and desperation merged with her conclusion that there was no other way out. Mira awaited their mutual ending.

Then, from somewhere far off in the distance, came a soft familiar voice. Mira heard Nona Rosa's gentle words whispering directly into Gina's soul. "This is not the answer, my love. There's another way."

Gina capped both bottles, put them back on her nightstand, lay her head back on her pillow, and fell into a deep sleep. In the depth of her slumber, she dreamed of a young woman riding a bicycle down a snowy street. The young woman had a hard time keeping her bike upright trying to ride through the deep snow. She looked down into the basket attached to the handlebars of her bike. Her eyes met with the eyes of a newborn baby swaddled in pink blankets. She felt the heavy weight of the responsibility she bore.

The next day, Gina sat in the waiting room of the abortion clinic. She'd passed the initial physical exam and waited for her "procedure." Her heart ached, but she could cry no more. Inside, nestled in her little clump of cells, Mira felt frightened and confused. She was awash in ambivalence. She didn't want to be a burden to Gina, but she felt excited to return. Before Gina discovered her, Mira felt certain of that. She had no hesitation and wanted to take her next steps. But now, she swirled in Gina's confusion and anxiety. Gina wanted to send her back. Mira knew her father was far away and didn't know she existed. Mira concluded that she was alone and unwanted and had made a mistake wanting to return. She wanted to leave.

"Hey! HEY! Wake up from your trance! I'm still here!" Nona reminded Mira.

"What?" Mira shook the cobwebs of confusion from her psyche.

"I'm still here . . . you forgot."

"Oh, yeah . . . you. So what now?"

"Well, that's your call. Are you open to a suggestion?" Nona ventured.

"Try me."

"There's a piece of business from another ending that's getting in the way here. Unfortunately, something happened before that keeps you from releasing the shock and shame you inherited from Gina when she discovered she was pregnant with you."

"Business? Another ending? Before?"

"Yes. Business from a previous beginning and ending to resolve. When you do, you can return to the original intention you set at your beginning of this time."

"You're talking gibberish. I have absolutely no idea what you mean."

"I know. The problem is that Gina's shock and shame obliterated your memory of the discussion we had before you returned."

"Last discussion we had? I don't remember any last discussion. We never talked like this before. I feel like we're going around in circles."

"We are. That's what happens when we have unfinished business from our past lives. Until we get it resolved, we keep going around in circles. It sucks."

Mira never heard such words out of her Nona. "Past lives? You know I don't believe in that woo-woo bullshit."

Nona disregarded Mira's last statement. "Your soul connected to an earlier lifetime that has unfinished business. That attachment remains and needs attention. You set an intention with me before you entered this beginning. It was completely your idea. I had nothing to do with it. It was your idea to come back, not mine. You wanted to heal the unfinished business and finally detach from that lifetime. But you got so wrapped up in Gina's feelings when she discovered you existed that you forgot what we discussed. It's about that life long ago in the forest, when you left the little one you birthed in the hot springs to die."

"Brought with me? The little one I birthed? I birthed no one! I would never leave a baby to die in a hot spring!" Mira shrieked in panic.

"Mira, it'll be all right," Nona said in a soothing tone. "Try to relax. It wasn't you. Let me explain. Wisps of our past embodiments travel with us from life to life, like ghosts camped out in the back of our closet. They patiently wait for a chance to express themselves. If we're not aware of them and unable to release them, they contaminate the spirit of our present lifetime. So the ghost of the girl from your time in the forest tagged along through your many endings and beginnings and arrived with you here in the one that just ended."

"What are you talking about? I already told you I never lived in a forest. I never birthed a baby." After a pause, Mira's voice softened, and her protestations weakened. "There's nothing I can do about it now, anyway."

Nona waited patiently as Mira quieted, and her energy dropped into a deeper state of consciousness. As she did, and as the unremembered became remembered, the image sharpened and emerged from a distant mist. And she knew it to be true.

With the memory now clear as fine crystal, Mira understood that she had spent a lifetime as the girl of the forest and that she had carried her throughout many lifetimes. Together, they carried the deep feeling that had no name but now carried a more severe sensation: shame. The forest girl carried her shame beyond her last breath, bequeathing it to all the spirits that followed her. And the emerald-green shards of light that had fallen from her soul into the waters of the hot springs remained in the forest to this very day. That green light embodied her heart and self-respect. Understanding the importance of those soul pieces, Mira felt their absence from her own soul and her need to recover them.

While Mira struggled to integrate the forest girl's experience, Nona continued, "The forest girl lived so very long ago and changed into a more advanced being. She did not understand guilt and shame and had no words for what she felt, but those feelings washed over her when she dropped her newborn child into the hot springs. She sensed she'd done something wrong, something for which she could not forgive herself.

"The two of you are not one, Mira. You are a separate being now, and it is not your job to carry her guilt and shame. Perhaps you can help her release the shame she carried and learn self-forgiveness so you don't have to carry it for her anymore. Help her reclaim her lost sense of pride in herself and find her heart again."

And with that, Mira returned and sat with the forest girl at her ending as she took her last breath. She cradled her hand and spoke to her in soft tones, reaching into the deepest part of her soul: "You didn't know. No one could teach you. You're an innocent child of the universe. Now is the time to release yourself from the sadness and self-recrimination you carry. You can move into the light of the universe and the Mystery beyond all Mysteries with purity and pride. You and I will live many lifetimes together —expanding our understanding and healing. Forgive yourself. You didn't know. Look up into the light of the Mystery. Let yourself go into the light in peace."

And as the forest girl's soul returned to and merged with the eternal light of the universe, emerald-green shards of pure energy lifted from the waters of the hot springs into the light and returned her and Mira's soul to wholeness.

"Wow!" Nona's eyebrows rose. "I couldn't have done that better myself. So now that you've taken care of that piece of unfinished business, is there something you want to say to that soul inhabiting the new being growing inside of Gina?"

Without hesitation, Mira continued to channel the wisdom of the universe, "Little Mira, you've chosen this life and this mother. You have every right to be here now and live this life fully. Her shame is not your shame! Her fear is not your fear! You're a child of the universe. She serves as your transport vessel into your life! You're a product of love and youth. This is your opportunity to heal and complete your mission."

"Whoa, you're on a roll here." Nona's grin lit up her face. "Anything else?"

Mira's spirit brimmed with a newfound passion. She shouted, "I want to live, Gina! Please forgive yourself and be proud of yourself. Trust your intuition. You and I have much to teach each other. Martin loves you and will love me. Please honor the universe's decision for you to be my mother, for Martin to be my father, and for me to be your child."

As the spirit of Nona and Mira observed from high above, Gina rose from her chair in the waiting room of the women's clinic and ran out the front door and down the street. As she did, Mira's energy field glowed bright red, and Nona's energy field sparkled in a rainbow of color.

~

Below, in Mira's condo, the female EMT performing chest massages on Mira's vacated body finally spoke: "I had a noticeable flutter of a heartbeat there for a moment, but it was irregular and only lasted about ten seconds. I'm continuing compressions, but she's still unresponsive. What do you think?"

"I don't know what to think," the dark-skinned EMT uttered to no one in particular. "It's just so sad . . . I think she's gone. I'm getting ready to call it."

| 24 |

Mira sat in the tangle of her faded pink bicycle and the garbage can with which she'd just collided. Her piercing laugh echoed back up the alleyway she'd just traveled. Her excited eyes searched for the powerful man with the deep voice who'd guided her on her very first bike ride. But seeing no one, Mira's soul ached for her lost father.

She gazed out over Elliott Bay from the balcony of the coffee shop, quietly sobbing to her Nona. "Why did you take him away from me? Why did you let Gina lie to me all those years about his being dead? I could've had him in my life if she'd told me the truth."

"Bring us two more cups of tea, please," Nona said to the young barista behind the counter. "We'll be here for a while."

The barista had been watching the two old ladies as they sat across from each other at their table, one crowned with reddish salt-and-pepper locks pulled into a single braid down the middle of her back, the other with silver-white braids streaked in faded red carefully woven into two long strands. Now, their teacups and plates littered with scone crumbs sat empty before them. They spoke in quiet tones for millennia, punctuated by long bouts of reflective silence or spikes of sharp retort.

Even though she'd asked before, Mira blurted out once again, "Tell me the truth: Are you God?"

Nona practically snorted. "Okay, let's get this straight right now! Pronouns and titles don't work here, but I'll try, anyway. 'We' are pure formless energy, so 'you' and 'I' really don't exist. 'Us' and 'we' are a stretch, but come closer. If you must continue to think in dualistic terms, perhaps this fits best: 'I' am the Divine Mother of all that is. 'I' birthed the universe from the nothingness that was. Perhaps think of me as the Mother of all Mothers, the uterus of all uteruses. I transmute formless into form, and yet I am formless."

Mira fell silent for a while, then retorted. "So that made absolutely no sense. All I know is that Nona called you God, and now you sit with me as Nona."

"I came to you in this form so we could have this conversation. 'I' am whatever you imagine me to be. Would you have preferred trying to wrap your head around all this by sitting with that bearded old White dude your ancestors dreamed up? The concept of 'God' is just a figment of small-minded imaginations. You could think of me like a cosmic womb or like a beehive, where the feminine creates, and the masculine protects and assists. In the hive, a male drone fertilizes a young queen before she enters the hive. That completes his work, and he and the other males live outside the hive. Inside, female worker bees serve the queen and build the hive. The feminine creates the container and the colony. In the universe's container, the alchemy of divine feminine energy continually moves formless into form and back to formless again."

"So who created that form of God Michelangelo painted in the Sistine Chapel? All of his paintings and sculptures depict God as an old man with flowing white hair and a beard."

Nona's eyes flashed lightning bolts for an instant before she said, "You've heard the expression 'follow the money?' Pope Julius II commissioned Michelangelo in 1503 to paint the ceiling of the Sistine Chapel. At the Pope's direction, Michelangelo depicted God as an old White dude with flowing hair and a beard with his right arm and hand outstretched to touch the fingertip of Adam. If you look closely, they draped his left arm around the single female figure in the picture. She is a young woman with small, uncovered breasts. She looks at 'God' with awe and fear in her eyes. It appears to be a gesture of ownership and dominance over the feminine. Angelic cherubs surround the two of them, all predictably male. All are naked save for 'God.' They covered his genitals—if he possessed any—while they exposed others of modest size. Everyone, including Adam, the woman, and the cherubs, seem to carry the shame of their sex exposed for all to see. By the 1500s, the church had converted most developed societies into patriarchies. So Michelangelo did not create the image of God in the image of the Creator; he created 'him' in the church's image." Nona took a moment to calm herself while she and Mira sipped their tea in silence for a while.

"That doesn't help me understand why Dad left me and why Gina made up a story that he'd died. Someone or something set that up, didn't they? Someone or something controls all of this, don't they?"

"I guess it's easier to believe some evil mastermind is at work controlling all that happens to us when terrible things happen that deeply hurt us. Perhaps we don't suffer as much if we believe we are all victims with no power or influence over what happens to us. But your father and mother made all their decisions themselves. Your father decided to join the army and become a warrior. He joined the special forces and put himself in harm's way, knowing he had a family back home. And when he became brutally wounded, his pride caused him to decide to leave his family and make up the story he had died. And your mother decided to keep his secret all those years until she could keep it no longer. They were like children themselves, without much guidance or knowledge."

Mira remained silent.

"Those decisions were the work of the humans involved, not Gods. Two forces are always at work in this world: those of the universe and those of embodied living beings. They operate independently of and in consort with one another. No magical wizard hides behind a curtain, pulling ropes and levers, controlling all that happens. Dorothy had to travel all the way to Oz, facing many tests along the way to learn that what she was seeking was inside herself all along. Back when your father was injured, and your parents made up the story he'd died, did you make up your own story about why he'd left you? When you were small, did you create your own conclusions about what your father's leaving really meant about you, and did you create your own decisions about how to cope with his being gone?"

Mira's spirit remained quiet for a moment before she answered. "I guess since I didn't have the actual story, I figured I didn't matter—that I wasn't important. Maybe I decided I was bad, perhaps a burden. Maybe I was in the way or not lovable. I was defective, or . . ."

Nona interrupted Mira's barrage on herself. "Yes, you see? You started hating yourself. Even though Gina made up the story that Martin died in a war and you could have believed his absence had nothing to do with you, you still believed it was your fault."

"Well, he hadn't come home to me. So it must have been because of me."

"So even if you had known the truth back then, you would have blamed yourself?"

Their tea was getting cold. Nona asked the barista for more boiling water.

Her voice softened. Quietly she said, "Blaming yourself is easier, isn't it?"

"Are you crazy? Easier? Easier than what?"

"Think about it," Nona said. "What else might it be?"

Without warning, somber thunderheads laden with grief blew into Mira's heart, generating a black storm of sorrow. Formless tears streamed from her tortured spirit. Pure, perfect pain cracked from the depths of her soul, sending magnificent silver-blue streaks of northern lights flashing across the deep midnight-blue sky around them.

Distracted by her cosmic grief, Mira didn't notice the tiny glowing emerald-green orb that appeared in the distance streaking toward them. It caught her attention once it grew closer and bigger and brighter. Finally, it stopped, hovering bright and huge, right next to them. It vibrated at supersonic speed and cast brilliant emerald light to the distant reaches of the universe. Once again, Mira heard that deep voice and felt that familiar powerful hand at the small of her back. The vibration calmed a bit, and pure love enveloped her completely.

"Mira, my leaving had nothing to do with you," her father's voice said, "and I never stopped loving you. My love for you is boundless, timeless, and complete. I've been keeping something you left behind with me that day in the hospital when I began my journey back into the infinite light of the universe. I never wanted it in the first place, but you left it with me in love. It helped me on my journey here, but it doesn't belong to me, and you need it for yourself. I tried returning it to you many times, without success. I've been taking good care of it until your return. Perhaps now is the time."

A small beam of pale-green light slowly crept out from the orb of her father's spirit. Mira tried to cast it aside, attempting to send it back to its source, but the ray deepened in color and penetrated further and stronger. The grief that connected her to her father dissolved with the infusion of deep-emerald-green energy he sent to her.

But without grief, she thought, what will connect us?

"Please stop blaming and degrading yourself, Mira. You're not as powerful as you believe. We've always been together, and we'll always stay connected. You're not responsible for our last separation, and neither am I. The other possibility is that we completed our last connection and may travel together again soon. We must believe in the Mystery beyond all Mysteries. But for now, it's time for you to take your heart energy back. You can't move on without it."

Reassured by her father's words, Mira began taking her heart's energy back into her spirit, allowing it to return to her. As she embraced its vibration, the heartache and pain permeating her spirit dissolved and fell away. Love and acceptance for herself filled her. Her spirit glowed bright green.

With the energy transfer complete, Martin's spirit kissed Mira's spirit on her forehead. Then, the orb moved silently off into the distance, returning to the Source. Mira watched with a feeling of deep peace and love for her father and herself. She felt the blue-green thread stretching from her energy field to his, along with the strength of their connection. She trusted that for all time, it would connect her to the infinite Source of all that is, all that ever was, and all that ever will be.

And then all was still . . . all was still.

| 25 |

"You already know everything about the boy who raped me at that house party when I was fourteen, don't you?" Mira asked.

"No, not everything," Nona said. "Tell me about it."

They sat together on a tufted leather seat in the womb of the VIP gondola of Seattle's Great Wheel. The city built the popular tourist attraction in 2012, balanced at the tip of Pier 57 on the Seattle waterfront. The massive ride towers 175 feet over Puget Sound, allowing patrons to view the ferry and tourist boats lazily plying the bay's waters, the bustling piers to the north and south, and the business towers rising from the hills of the city center behind it.

Their car swayed gently as it came to a stop and remained at the pinnacle of its arc high above the frigid water below. The other forty-one cars lounged, empty of humans, as did the surrounding docks, piers, buildings, and streets. The city had become a ghost town save for Nona and Mira. They gazed out toward Bainbridge Island to the west and beyond to the snow-capped range of mountains rising above the Olympic Peninsula. They said nothing to each other for a time.

Mira eventually broke the silence. "I never told a soul, not even Mel, and didn't fight it. I've always been so confused about what happened there. Why didn't I scream for help or push him off me? Maybe I wanted it. I had a grown-up body, so I thought maybe it was the thing to do next. My friends were right downstairs. Other people were doing it in other parts of the house. I didn't know the boy and didn't want to have sex with him. I was just there to party and have some fun. He kept giving me alcohol, and people were passing joints around nonstop. How I ended up in that room, I'll never know. Hell, I never met the dude and didn't even know his name! I must have passed out, and he stripped off my jeans and underpants. I don't remember. He pushed inside me before I knew it. I just lay there and took it. He finished fast, and it was over."

Mira fell silent for a moment, shocked by the graphic details she'd shared. "Mom told me never to have sex with someone I didn't know or who didn't care about me. Back then, I knew how it would've hurt you, so I couldn't even tell you about it. But the shame was too much for me to bear."

Nona remained silent.

"Can you ever forgive me?" Mira asked. Her shame and sadness filled the gondola like a heavy fog gathering in the deep valleys between the peaks of the Cascade Mountains on a chilled fall morning.

Nona reached out and cupped Mira's face in her loving hands. She looked deeply into her granddaughter's eyes with the gentleness and wisdom of all grandmothers from the beginning of time. "Can you ever forgive yourself? I love you without condition. I accept you without judgment. But, ask yourself this: might something have happened even earlier in my life that influenced the events of the party?"

Mira frowned thoughtfully. "I wondered about that myself, especially after reading about people who had memories of traumatic events after something else triggered them. But I can't use something like that as an excuse for letting that boy fuck me when I was fourteen. I decided to go to the party and drink alcohol and didn't have to go into that room with him alone. I could have pushed him off me and screamed for help."

"Yes, everything you said about making excuses is true," Nona said. "We all must ultimately take responsibility for our decisions and our actions. But the word 'responsibility' doesn't mean the same as 'blame.' That boy took sexual liberties without your permission while you were drunk. Why did he serve whiskey to a fourteen-year-old girl he'd never met and have sex with you without knowing you? And why did he leave you there when he finished without making sure you got home all right? He could have shown you the same basic human decencies and considerations someone would show a friend. So shouldn't we hold the boy responsible for his decisions and his actions that day as well?" Nona paused for a moment, then added, "How about we quit all this talking and go back to retrieve what you left there without knowing?"

"Left there?"

"Yes."

"I'm confused."

Mira and Nona dissolved into the energy field of the collective and regrouped on the ceiling of the bedroom containing Mira's fourteen-year-old self. She sat alone on the bed, drunk and in shock after being raped. She'd pulled her underwear and jeans back onto her slight body. Her image in the mirror showed her that the smoothed hair and carefully applied makeup she'd arrived at the party with had now become tangled and rubbed from her face. Her features appeared innocent, and her eyes carried the confusion and fear of her youth. Tears stained her shirt, but her body didn't cry. She felt deeply injured but not hurt. Although devastated, she showed no emotion. Her throat longed to scream, but she remained mute. Her muscles strained to hit something, but her arms remained frozen in paralysis. She was numb, traumatized throughout her core.

"You must speak to her soul, Mira. In this terrible moment of chemical intoxication and the shock of physical attack, she is embedding false conclusions into her core operating system about who she is. Based on those false conclusions, she is creating permanent decisions about how to cope with her life. See the bright-orange shards of her soul that split apart from her and gathered around her feet? If not recovered, she will leave them there forgotten for all time. She needs a wise feminine adult to guide her. She is drowning in shame. Help her!"

Mira looked down on her younger self with an overwhelming sense of disgust. She hated this younger form—skinny and flat-chested, her thick hair curly and tangled. She hated her nose and thought her eyes were too big. Insecure and shy, she was naïve and unsophisticated. She judged herself to be ugly and un-interesting. She wanted nothing to do with this four-teen-year-old version of herself.

Sensing Mira's brutal judgments of the girl sit-ting injured below them, Nona whispered, "Look past her physical countenance and immature personality and peer deep into her heart and her soul. She is only fourteen years old and just experienced a horrible event in her young life. Her father abandoned her, and her mother neglected her. Look past what you see and soften your judgments of her. Look into the vulner-able child that she is. Let yourself see her through my eyes now."

Mira used Nona's eyes to see the young girl sit-ting on the bed below. She looked past the shame and judgments she'd formed from the events of that day. With Nona's eyes, she witnessed her true heart and soul. And, when she did, she felt a complete, undeni-able, and fierce love for her younger self.

"Speak to her, Mira. She needs you now more than ever before."

The spirit of Mira gently descended to address her younger self. The two melded together along with those of Nona and even those beyond. Mira opened a channel of healing energy from the hearts and minds of her ancient ancestors to address the broken spirit of the girl sitting on the bed:

"Hear me, young one, listen carefully to me. You are the innocent embodiment of the Mystery beyond all Mysteries. You are one with the universe. The drama acted out earlier in this room does not define you. This is one incident in a lifetime of many. It comes to you as a silver platter brimming with the potential for great learning and transmutation. You can release yourself from the shame and devastating conclusions you are making now: that you are solely to blame for this; that this event has soiled and damaged you for life forever; that you are now defective and destined to live a lifetime of shame and addiction based on a singular event and decision that occurred during a tough time in your childhood. As you release the conclusions and decisions you created then, you can heal from this and all other traumas that befell you."

While young Mira allowed the channeled energy of the universe to enter her, Nona witnessed the shards of glowing-orange energy lifting and merging back into Mira's teenage body. Mira felt her soul pieces restoring themselves, and the entire room glowed bright orange, reflecting the light of her creativity, along with her life-force energy and her innocent sexuality.

And, in that instant, the room emptied.

| 26 |

Nona and Mira sat on a park bench at Madrona Beach, silently looking out over Lake Washington. Mira had passed the bench regularly on her ritual runs along the trail that followed the shoreline there. Today, the chill of the cold winter day challenged their lush woolen coats. Above them, foreboding dark grey cumulus clouds stacked on top of each other, preparing to jettison their cargo of wet snow. Most times, the snow melted quickly with Seattle's temperate climate, but today's sub-freezing temperature predicted an accumulation.

"Nona, there's something I have to tell you I've kept secret my entire life."

Nona replied, "What is it, dear one?"

"I'm so ashamed; I'm so ashamed . . ." Huge tears welled up in Mira's eyes and began spilling from her in rivulets.

"Tell me, dear one, what is it you carry?"

"It happened after Mom brought that monster into our house. Dad had died, or at least that's what she told me, and she was lonely. She needed help keeping the house together, and a friend gave her the name of a handyperson. He came over to look at the house one day, and she hired him on the spot to fix our deck. I think I was about seven years old."

Mira went quiet.

"Go on, dear."

"I heard mom yell out in the backyard while I played in my room, and the sounds she made I'd never heard before. It made me think someone's hurting her. I ran out of the house and didn't know where she was. I came around the house beside the shed in the backyard and heard weird noises from inside the shed. Most of me didn't want to see what was happening in there, but it was like I had to see. I peeked around the corner of the door and saw Mom perched up on the workbench with her dress pulled up to her shoulders.

"I saw him standing facing her with his pants on the floor around his ankles. He held mom's legs by her ankles and had them spread apart. I could see what was between his legs, and he was pushing it in and out of her. I was just a little kid and had never seen sex before. It scared me, and it was gross, but I couldn't look away. They were both sweating and making gross sounds. I couldn't breathe. Mom was panting and squealing, and he was groaning and cursing. I don't know how long it went on, but I couldn't move or take my eyes away from what I saw. Finally, he pushed hard into Mom one last time, and she screamed out. He moaned out loud, and they both went limp on each other. Then he pulled out of her and dropped her legs. They never saw me, and I turned and ran back to my room."

Nona let Mira rest for a while before she responded. "That must have been terrifying for you to see that, young as you were. What did you think? What did you feel?"

"I'd never witnessed sex before, and no one had told me about it. I didn't know men had that thing and didn't know what it did. It terrified me because I thought he was hurting her, but I felt excitement in my body when they both came. The entire scene totally confused me."

Mira figured Nona already knew what was coming next.

"But that wasn't the worst of what I need to tell you."

"When I was much younger, there was a wonderful dream that came to me frequently. I dreamt I was with my father on a camping trip. We'd taken our gear up across the North Cascades Highway to Lake Diablo and pitched our tent next to the lake. It was the most beautiful place I'd ever seen. They built Diablo Dam to provide electric power to Seattle, and the lake formed behind it. Glacial rock particles in the water turned it the color of iridescent turquoise when the sunlight struck it. I'd seen nothing like the blue-green shimmering light that reflected from the lake. I dreamed that aliens from another universe transported the water there at the beginning of time.

"After dark, Dad and I made s'mores and told stories by the campfire. Dad tried to freak me out by telling scary stories and making monster faces reflected in the campfire. But even as young as I was, I knew he was playing and felt safe when he tucked me into my sleeping bag at night. He always checked the tent and especially my sleeping bag for snakes. He told me that sometimes snakes would slither into a camp tent to find a spot to hide when no one noticed, but he always made sure the tent was safe before I got in.

"But then, in my twenties, the dream turned into a nightmare. I dreamt that, after I'd fallen asleep in my sleeping bag, I'd wake up in the middle of the night choking. I couldn't breathe. My throat was completely closed, and I felt something pushing into my mouth and down my throat. I opened my eyes for just a second and saw the tail of a gigantic snake curling in front of my face, trying to get in my mouth. I woke up in a complete panic, drenched in sweat and gulping for air. It was horrible, and it happened almost every night.

"It got so bad I went to see a therapist about it. She asked if perhaps I had an umbilical cord wrapped around my neck at birth or had a near-drowning experience. How was I supposed to know? That's why I went to her, to find out. I went for a few sessions, waiting for her to ask me the obvious question—had anyone sexually abused me when I was growing up and pushed something into my mouth and throat? Since she never asked me directly, I assumed no one had."

"Do you think you knew but didn't want to believe it?" Nona asked.

"My body knew, but I guess my mind couldn't handle it," Mira replied. "I couldn't wrap myself around the truth. That son of a bitch got blind drunk one night, came into my room while I slept, and pushed his cock down my little throat. I know it now in every cell of my body!" Mira shouted in deep shock.

Mira and Nona sat in deafening silence, gazing into the deep-gunmetal gray of the Lake Washington water. Heavy snow fell around them, the cold chilling them to their core.

Finally, Nona said, "Unthinkable. I'm so sorry you had to endure that." She paused for a moment before continuing, wondering if it was too soon, "Might there be an important part of you that split off when he raped you?"

"Part of me that split off? What do you mean?"

"Sometimes, when something traumatic happens in our life, especially when we are very young, the only way we can survive the trauma is to block it out from our conscious memory. But, in doing so, we separate ourselves from an important part of our soul; we experience a soul split. Then later, we might receive a coded message that gives us a clue that we might be ready to heal the trauma. That's probably what your dream was about. Your subconscious mind showed you the snake to see if you were ready to deal with the rape. But no one was around when you had the dream to help you understand its deeper meaning. So now you can explore if the dream represents Sergie's attack. Think about it for a moment, Mira; if important parts of your soul split off when Sergei raped you, what might they have been?"

Mira didn't have to think about it long. "I lost my safety, my innocence, and my power. My first sexual experience was an oral rape that happened when I was seven. He forced it on me, and my mother didn't protect me. Most people get to choose their first sexual experience once they are older and have learned what sex is all about. That fucker stole my innocence, and no one protected me. Mom brought him into our home, and Dad had left. I had no protection and no power."

The falling snow gathered around their feet, like doilies of white lace, and piled high on their shoulders and thighs. Nona stretched out her arms, drawing a large circle into the sky over their heads. As she did, an invisible canopy formed above them, sheltering them from the cold, wet accumulation that continued to form beyond the boundary of their cover.

"I'm with you now, and you're safe," Nona said in reassuring tones. "There's a way to correct what happened that night and heal the harm done to you there. If you wish, we can go back together now and take care of the business that remains unfinished."

"Take care of the unfinished business? What the fuck are you talking about?"

"You said there was no one there to help or protect you. So I suggested we go back together and help her."

"You mean we could go back and kill that motherfucker?"

"I know you feel rage from the event, and that's understandable. But we can't change what happened. Changing history denies any learning that can take place. She needs help in understanding and dealing with what happened to her. So if you go back intending to heal, you can recover some of the soul parts you might have left there."

"Now you sound like that therapist I went to see." Mira mimicked in a sing-song of insincere empathy, "We have to learn how to understand and deal with the traumas we experienced in our childhood so we can heal and move on. How about we just cut off his dick and stuff it down his throat?"

Nona disregarded Mira's outburst. "I understand your rage with what he did to you that night. He had no right to attack you, and he should have paid dearly for his crimes against you. And, yes, your therapist should have checked for childhood sexual abuse. But, on a much higher level, what occurred that night in your bedroom was your karma and his karma, and each was separate from the other. You're responsible for dealing with the consequences it produced in your life, and he must deal with the consequences it produced in his life."

"The consequences it produced in his life? He got away absolutely free of charge! Mom never found out, and she continued living with that lowlife until she caught him cheating on her and threw him out. No one ever found out, and I ended up having nightmares my entire life and committing suicide."

"Where is Sergei now?" Nona asked.

"Mom told me she heard he fell off a roof he was working on and ended up paralyzed in a wheelchair. He tried to get her to take care of him, but by then, she'd wised up. I heard he died some years ago from cirrhosis of the liver."

Nona smiled. "The Mystery can deliver some powerful paybacks, huh?"

"I regret never telling Mom what he did to me, but I didn't remember it. I guess if I'd consciously remembered, I would have blamed her, and that wouldn't have been fair. But, of course, if she'd known, I'm sure she would've felt awful and blamed herself, anyway. So It wasn't her fault, either."

"You're right, Mira. Everything that happens to us in our embodied form is exactly what we need to grow to a higher plane. When we return to a disembodied state, as you are now, we can process and integrate the events of our lifetime. Blame and consequences are the stuff of being embodied. Consciousness and transformation happen when we enter the collective unconscious, the place where all disembodied souls live together."

"The collective unconscious?"

"Yes, where we are right now."

Although Mira didn't understand Nona completely, her words entered her at a level she'd never experienced before.

"If we blame Martin for abandoning you when you were so young, and blame Gina for bringing Sergei into your life, or if we go back and kill Sergei for raping you when you were little, or even stop him from raping you at all, we would stop all of you from your rightful evolutions, your movement to a higher state of being. As hard as it is to believe or stomach, it would even stop Sergei from reaching his potential for redemption. Tinkering with any of our past histories alters the course of the entire universe; it destroys the order of everything and stops our process of learning and growing."

When Nona's words completed their download into Mira's consciousness, she fell headlong into a vortex of turmoil. "So you're saying everything that happens to us is part of some master plan, and someone predetermines our entire existence. So we can't avoid wars and rapes and murders, right? And who the hell decides what to put in this master plan, anyway? Let's go stop him instead!"

"See how easy it is for that whole omnipotent God theory to creep back in?" Nona said. "'Predetermined' is too simple. It's so much more complex, more fluid than that. The universe serves up silver platters brimming with challenges for growth. There's no evil intent, no wizard behind a curtain pulling strings, just life as it unfolds. So it's best not to take what happens in our life personally, as if life has singled you out by some vengeful god-figure for punishment for reasons unknown to you."

"What you're saying is nuts!" Mira shouted. "You're just another figment of my dying mind, like that last dude you must have sent! You're a hallucination, and I want you to go away and leave me alone and let me finish dying!"

~

The EMTs had carefully transferred Mira's lifeless body from the floor of her condo onto an ambulance gurney. They snaked an intubation device from outside her lips, inside her mouth, over her tongue, past her epiglottis, around her vocal cords, and down into her trachea. While his partner continued her cadence of chest compressions, the dark-skinned EMT pushed methodically on the sides of the bag connected to the air tube that forced rhythmic breath into Mira's lungs.

"You need to call this one, Marty. She's been unresponsive for over thirty minutes. Calls are coming in, and they want us to finish up."

"Give me five more minutes. Then, if she's still unresponsive, we'll call it," Marty whispered. "She's just so fucking young."

~

As they watched the drama unfolding below them, Nona whispered, "If you're ready to move into the Light of the Universe, you can make that choice now. No one is keeping you here; it's been your choice all along. You can let go when you wish. There's no right or wrong in this place, no good or bad, no consequences to the choices you make here. This is a place for reflection and decision. Some believe it to be a place of cleansing and purification after spending their time embodied. Some bypass their work here only to move into the Light with ghosts from their life just lived still attached to their spirit. Perhaps you've truly finished your work now; only you can decide. Trust your inner knowing. We love and support you no matter what you decide."

A pillar of brilliant violet light descended over the park bench on which they sat as Nona spoke. It grew closer and wider and brighter until it towered above them and began to envelop them both. Mira's spirit felt a powerful magnetic pull of energy emanating from inside the light. Immediately she knew she'd made the right decision. She was ready to go. Trying to understand had exhausted her.

The pillar of light blazed blindingly bright. Mira felt herself rise into its core. A peace came over her as she'd never felt before. She floated up like a birthday balloon that had escaped from a child's wrist.

Mira peered up into the glowing light and looked into the faces of her known and unknown ancestors. They beckoned their welcome to her, silently inviting her to join them. Their energy of pure love assured her she was safe and cared for and that she could end the suffering of her embodied lifetime. She felt complete understanding and empathy for the decision she'd made. Her belief that her destiny was complete for this lifetime made her accepted by all who welcomed her.

Mira began merging with the light. Her energy and the energy of the universe danced together, braiding and intertwining with one another, becoming indiscernible from each other. Then, finally, she felt the joy and celebration of her return to the Mystery beyond all Mysteries.

She turned to take one quick look back to say goodbye. Nona grew smaller, still sitting on the park bench next to the lake. Her grandmother's arms reached out to the universe in supplication.

Thick snow gathered and glistened all around

her. Her face reflected all the golden light of pure grace and love that the universe offered.

As Mira turned her gaze back into the light, she briefly glimpsed the scene still reflected just behind Nona, her childhood bedroom with her little self in her bed suffering abuse. The little one clenched her eyes tightly against the excruciating pain, her body filled with terror and tension, and her innocent mind brimming with confusion and loneliness.

As she witnessed the scene, sadness and grief enveloped Mira. And she finally knew she wasn't ready for what lay beyond, not without the parts of her soul she'd left behind in that room. Suspended there in the universe's loving light, neither ascending nor descending, Mira cried out to her ancestors for guidance.

"Dear God in Heaven, please tell me what to do. I'm exhausted and desolate and can't do this alone. Give me your guidance and support." She fell onto her disembodied knees. "Please help me . . . please, please, please . . . help me," she cried out.

And there before her appeared the face of a great, great grandmother she'd never met and never known; her father Martin's great-grandmother. Slave traders had abducted her in Africa when she was fourteen and brought her to South Carolina on a slave ship in 1860. Her African name had been Duba. Then Duba gazed down on Mira from the light of the universe, her boot-black African skin glowing.

"Go back to her, Mira. Love her. Heal her. Guide her. She's an innocent child of the universe. Your dislike of her represents her shame and other shame you collected during your lifetime.

Now you can release that shame and love her unconditionally. She's all of us. If you abandon her now, you're abandoning yourself and abandoning all of us. Do this for yourself. Please do this for me and all those who came before you. And if you do this for yourself and me and all those who came before you, you will do this for all those who will come after you as well."

And so, with the blessings of her ancestors, Mira descended from the column of light.

"We'll need another cup of tea," Nona called over to the barista standing patiently behind the counter of the empty coffee shop. The clock on the wall sat motionlessly.

The sun had already set behind the Olympic Mountains to the west of Puget Sound, igniting the sky with flames of gold, apricot, and peach, interrupted by intermittent blots of withering gray clouds, all painting their colors on the snow-drenched mountains below. The conversation Nona was about to have with Mira would be intense.

"You said I could be with my seven-year-old self again if I wished. Why would I want to be with her?" Mira said. "She's a homely little kid with buck teeth, no father, and a slut for a mother. When Sergei attacked her, she didn't even scream or run out of the room. She's damaged goods. If she wants to survive at all, she has to suck it up, push all her rage, fear, and shame deep inside her; move on; and forget this ever happened. All I can think of is that I want to kill that bastard. He raped me as a child in my house while my mother slept in the room next to mine. Why did you let that happen to me? You fancy yourself the all-powerful creator of all that is, the so-called 'divine feminine, super uterus mumbo jumbo,' so why can't you use your powers to un-create what happened to me?"

Nona sipped her tea, deep in contemplation. She breathed in to the count of eight and breathed out to the count of eight, trying her best to center herself. Finally, she could contain herself no longer. "There you go again, spouting that crap you learned in Sunday school," she said. How could she possibly explain the entire workings of the universe in twenty-five words or less?

"Let's be clear here; I don't control all this. Remember, I just birthed it. Since you've never been a mother, you don't realize how little control a mother has over her children. If I were a child psychologist, I wouldn't know what to call the current stage that the world is in. Terrible twos? Adolescence? Crotchety old age? Your guess is as good as mine. Anyway, I don't run the universe like the CEO of Amazon or Microsoft. The universe possesses a clear-cut order of its own; the Earth circling the Sun and gravity holding everything down. We don't feel the solar system as it screams through the universe at 448,000 miles per hour, and yet here we sit sipping tea and eating scones in a coffee shop in the market. So much is predictable about embodied life on earth, like the seasons that allow people to grow crops and harvest them. Like human beings exerting free will and acting independently, deciding what they believe and how they want to behave in situations. That's part of the Great

Mystery. So I didn't cause your mother to bring Sergei into your house, and I didn't cause him to rape you; no one did. And I didn't choose the family you landed in; you did. That's just part of the mystery. And what happened there that night was a silver platter for you to figure out—and part of what you came to work on this time around."

Mira exploded. "Choose the family I landed in? Part of what I came here to work on? This time around? What are you talking about? Are you fucking crazy? Would I choose a mother who would bring an alcoholic rapist into the house and a father who would go off to fight in a war, get blown up, and never come home to be my father? And while we are talking about choosing, why in the hell would you choose to birth a world of pain and trauma, chaos and war, and insanity and death? Those are exactly the reasons I ended it all! And frankly, I don't want any part of it again."

"You still don't quite have it right," Nona retorted. "I birthed the entire universe and all that inhabits it from here to eternity. It's vast and complex. You don't even know 1 percent of it. So instead, you focus on particular aspects of the universe that directly influenced your human experience in excruciating ways. Most of what you describe are the inventions of men—war, violence, chaos, pain, trauma, rape. I don't believe the universe birthed those manifestations. They are the invention of masculine energy gone awry. They are not the nature of the feminine."

"Then why the fuck did you birth men?" Mira asked.

"Come on, Mira. How would chili taste with no cayenne? You could have joined a convent, right? Yes, I birthed men, but I never meant for women to sacrifice their agency to them. They made that decision all on their own. There was a time in most cultures when men revered women as goddesses and supported them as their leaders. Then, over time, men gained control over women and convinced them to cede their power to them. The world has been suffering the consequences of that for some time now. So please, never forget, I also birthed the air that you breathed, the wonderful foods that you ate, the fragrant cherry blossoms that bloomed along Lake Washington you ran under in the spring, the sunsets you admired from your beautiful home, and the love your father had for you and still has for you."

Mira fell quiet. The mention of her father shifted the mood of the discussion and brought a rain of tears from her heart. She realized how much she missed having him in her life.

"Then why did that bastard do it? I was only seven. Why did he ruin my life?"

"Ruin your life?"

"Yes, Goddammit! Sorry."

"Don't worry about it. People curse me every day in every language on earth. I'm used to it. No one ruined your life; you didn't remember why you came here long before Sergei did what he did."

"How do you know that?"

"You forget I know everything. Here's the hard part you're trying to integrate; your soul chose all of this. We discussed it before you came back this time. You said you wanted to grow, learn, reach a higher plane, become enlightened. You created your intention before you came back into embodiment."

"Wait! Just hold on a minute . . . what? We discussed all this before I came back into embodiment this time? We've been together before now and talked before?"

"Well, yes. Actually, we were, and are, and always have been, together because we are one. So try to let go of the notion of together and apart. It's like up and down, or in and out, trying to make everything relative to something else."

A sly smile curled across Nona's face as she ventured into the quicksand of trying to teach Mira about concepts that are perhaps unfathomable and unteachable, that all of life is a paradox with infinite potentiality.

"Let's try to get real here for a minute," Nona said. "I want you to try an experiment for me. I want you to scream so loud they can hear it all the way to the very edge of the universe. But I want you to scream this particular sentence: You ruined my life, you fucking asshole!"

"Such terrible language, Nona." Mira chuckled. "When I was a kid, you would have sent me to my room for that."

"That was there, and this is here," Nona said. "Are you willing to try it?"

Mira wound up and screamed to the edge of the universe, "You fucking asshole, you ruined my life!"

The words reverberated throughout space and time and reechoed back to them

"How does that make you feel?" Nona asked.

"Angry, and I feel a sense of release. But then sad and hopeless."

"Now try screaming these words even louder: I will not allow what you did to me to define who I am!"

"Say that again?" Mira asked.

Nona repeated more softly this time. "I will not allow what you did to me to define who I am. Try it."

Mira drew in a hurricane of wind and screamed out beyond the far reaches of the universe, "I will not allow what you did to me to define who I am!"

They heard the echo coming back to them.

Mira repeated the sentence to herself with each echo that returned and let the words enter her soul:

I will not allow what you did to me to define who I am.

I will not allow what you did to me to define who I am.

I will not allow what you did to me to define who I am.

"Try to think of it this way, Mira. For every question in life, there are three potential answers, not just two: things are true, or not true, or not not true."

Mira sat in befuddled silence for a moment, allowing what she'd just heard to soak in like the maple syrup Nona used to pour onto her pancakes on Sunday mornings. Then she lit up and responded with excited but false confidence. "Wait. I know what's going on here. You're trying to trick me by talking gibberish.

Look, if something is not true, it has to be false. There are only two possibilities: true and false. I took Intro to Philosophy, and we learned deductive logic."

Nona sat in silence.

Mira glazed over for a moment as she feebly continued to attempt to explain the universe back to Nona. "Okay, so false and not true must be the same, right? So if something is not true and is not false, it has to be true, right?"

"Really?" Nona asked. "Are you sure that's right?"

Mira's thoughts overheated and began to smolder. "Wait. So you're saying if something is not not true, it's neither true nor false. Are you saying it's something else we don't understand or haven't experienced yet?" Mira asked with a sense of conviction, even though she wasn't sure what she'd just said.

"I think she's getting it!" Nona shouted. "Do you remember the question you asked?"

Confused, Mira asked, "Which question?"

"You asked, 'Then why did he do it? Why did he ruin my life?'"

"Oh yeah, that question."

Nona continued, "So what if it's not true that he ruined your life?"

"Because it's the truth. My life became ruined after he did what he did."

"Is it what he did that ruined your life, or did your belief that he ruined your life ruin your life? You said you took Intro to Philosophy in college and learned deductive logic. Could we not deduce that when you formed the belief that the rape ruined your life, that the belief ruined your life rather than the rape itself? That's how not not true works, by considering that unknown possibilities may exist that create our reality."

Mira thought for a moment before blurting out, "then it means there may be something else I don't understand or haven't encountered yet."

Nona sipped her tea and nodded in approval.

Mira continued with muted excitement. "Well, you can't expect me to understand why he did what he did or to accept it or forgive him for doing it. Of course, I wish he'd paid a severe price for what he did to me. But I'm willing to consider that I don't yet fully understand that it's not not true, that he ruined my life."

Nona listened carefully to the last sentence Mira posited. While it seemed perfectly nonsensical, it made perfect sense to Nona; Mira was ready to consider that it was possible that the rape had not ruined her life.

"Do you remember what you said about that innocent child who suffered such a violent attack in her sleep? You said, 'She's a homely little kid with buck teeth, no father, and a slut for a mother. She didn't even scream or run out of the room. She's damaged goods. If she survives at all, she has to suck it up, push all her rage, fear, and shame deep inside of her, move on, and forget this ever happened.'"

Mira listened to her own words repeated back to herself, shocked to hear her violent verbal attack on herself. She couldn't believe she'd formed such damning judgments about herself as a mere seven-year-old child.

"Those words have been guiding your life and your decisions since that awful night. Now you can consider that those damning judgments are not not true. Perhaps you can introduce yourself to someone you didn't know existed; you can call her your wise woman. She's been asleep inside you since the beginning of time. Either you lost track of her somewhere along the way, or no one introduced you to her. Your wise woman is the very highest part of your spirit, the most mature and wise aspect of yourself. She's there to help you through the most challenging times. Try calling on your wise woman right now. All you have to do is say, 'I call on my wise woman now for help and guidance,' and she'll come to you without fail."

Mira and Nona meditated briefly before calling upon the spirit of the wise woman in both of them to come forth. Then, when they felt her presence before them, they asked, "Oh, wise woman, what did little Mira need more than anything else when she experienced the horrible events at the hands of a violent pedophile? What will happen to her if she forms the self-damning belief that she caused this event, and what will happen if she blames herself and damns herself to hell as a ruined human being and continues to carry those beliefs with her throughout her life? What is likely to become of her?"

Mira and Nona sat in silence as their wise women contemplated the question.

Mira's wise woman finally said, "She's likely to bury the event deep in her subconscious along with all the feelings she has about it. As a result, she may live a life full of sorrow and stress, feel unfulfilled and confused, turn to drugs and alcohol, and perhaps even impulsively commit suicide one night in her condo without knowing why."

"Oh," Nona said.

Mira fell silent.

"And might she be able to form other beliefs and decisions about the horrible events she experienced at the hands of a violent pedophile?" Nona asked.

Mira's wise woman replied, "She could also believe that she's an innocent child of the universe who did nothing to warrant such horrible treatment and neglect. She could feel the depth of her anger, hurt, sadness, and pain without engaging in self-recrimination, and she could release all those feelings and engage in healthy self-care and healing practices throughout her life."

Nona nodded. "Interesting."

Mira felt her disembodied spirit relax a bit. If she still had lungs, she would've taken a deep breath and slowly exhaled.

| 28 |

The barista standing over by the pastry bar signaled his growing frustration with a heavy sigh. Mira noticed he'd started fidgeting after he'd brought their last cup of tea. Then, finally, he came straight over to their table and said, "I've got to close now. I've got to lock up."

Nona sighed. "I've really got to get going now too, Mira. Of course, I'd love to keep visiting, but I believe we've done all we can for now."

"But you can't go now . . . I'm not ready yet."

"Mira, please understand, you brought me here in this form so you can discern and integrate the life you just left. What is not not true is that I am you, and you are me—we are one, have always been one, and will be one forever."

And with that pronouncement, Nona stood, leaned over, placed the softest kiss on Mira's forehead she'd ever felt, and vaporized like steam from a hot cup of tea.

If disembodied energy could have a full-blown panic attack, Mira had one. She was alone and scared. Nona had not prepared her for this moment.

"I was waiting for her to leave. Why don't I finish cleaning up, and you and I get out of here?"

The voice behind her startled her back to the present. Mira looked up to see the barista who had moved beside her at the table. For a dying spirit delusion, he was cute and distracted her from Nona's abrupt departure. "Excuse me," she asked, "but who are you?"

"People call me Split. Before I got here, I was Shadow. I like Split better. What do you like?"

Mira didn't know what to think. But then, old thoughts began dancing in her psyche. "I like Split; it's cool. I've never heard it before. How did you get it?"

"A guy who was traveling through here came in and asked for a split-shot latte. You know, one shot of caf and one shot of decaf. I made it for him, and he drank it right down. While I was making his drink, he told me he'd been a shrink before stopping here. When he talked to me, it was as if he told me his total life story in one sentence. It was weird. I don't remember a word he said to me, but the one sentence told me everything about him. When he came in the next day, he called me Split.

"He said, 'Hey, Split, you know what I like, right?' So I made his drink, and, when he left, he told me to make sure I looked up what split meant, like it was important. I figured he just meant about the latte, but maybe he was talking about something else. He never came in again, and I never looked it up. But I decided I liked the name, so I started going by Split. You get it?"

Mira dodged his question with some small talk.

"So, how long have you been here?"

Split's attention seemed to wander off. "Long? What's 'long'?" he mused.

Talking with Split confused Mira. Old feelings washed over her. Ghosts of romantic fantasies mixed with sexual energy vibrated through her. Memories overtook her:

When she'd been in her body, she never knew why it responded the way it did. No one taught her how female sexual energy felt or how to manage it. She discovered masturbation on her own, and it didn't trigger memories of Sergei. Touching herself was fun and relaxing once she understood the magic of her body parts. Gina thought she'd misplaced her vibrator when she found it missing, but Mira had pilfered it and stashed it safely in her room.

Mira also didn't know about addiction. They'd talked about it a bit in health class and even asked kids to sign a sobriety contract. Everyone treated it as a joke and laughingly signed them. The teachers never asked about or invited them to talk about addicts in their families—the alcoholics coming home drunk late at night, waking up the entire house, falling down drunk, spending the family's money on booze or drugs, leaving little for food and clothing, perhaps becoming physically and emotionally violent toward their spouses or children. They never mentioned those realities. They didn't even give a message of help or treatment when problems with addiction arose, either for the addict or for the family. The only message offered was the practice of abstinence.

When she was eleven, Mira smoked cigarettes with her friends behind a garage close to school. By the time she was twelve, they'd used unsupervised homes when parents weren't around. They raided their liquor cabinet, drank their booze, and replaced the missing alcohol with water. By eighth grade, they cut school early to attend house parties at high schoolers' houses that were open to having younger girls there. Parents were too stupid to figure out what was happening or didn't care. Gina's house was one of them. One house party resulted in Mira's rape.

By high school, a cavernous depression slept in Mira's psyche. It had invaded many of her friends' psyches too. A girl in her sophomore class went home one night, took twenty oxys from her parent's medicine cabinet, washed it down with whiskey straight from the bottle, and hung herself from her closet doorknob with one of her scarves. An announcement came over the school intercom the next morning that counselors would be available in the cafeteria all day for any student who wanted to talk about what had happened. The school held a memorial service a week later in the gymnasium, where the grim-faced parents and siblings spoke publicly about their loss. Afterward, the students released balloons into the sky outside. Everyone wept and embraced one another and then went home. After that day, Mira didn't remember the dead girl's name ever being mentioned again at school, as her own sorrow and grief moved into her well of ever-deepening depression.

When she was thirteen, Mira could identify

most of the prescription-drug bottles in the medicine cabinets of her friends' houses. She learned what would get her high or fill her with bliss—codeine, oxycodone, hydrocodone, tramadol, morphine, hydromorphone, fentanyl; they were all right there for the taking. When she wanted uppers, she would steal her friends' ADHD medication—Vyvanse, Ritalin, Concerta, Adderall, Strattera. Many times, they easily found their parents' stash of street drugs—weed, coke, meth, even crack. She was so high on alcohol and pills the night that boy raped her, she blacked out the entire episode.

She learned the boys always expected sex. After the rape, Mira's cravings for male sexual contact became addictive. Her need to connect with masculine energy was insatiable, and she didn't understand why. Getting high was a prerequisite. She learned ways to satisfy the cravings that seemed interesting and exciting. What ultimately became addictive was getting boys off. The power she felt when a boy came was intoxicating. The control she felt over them blocked out the offensive smell of their bodies and their fluids.

She started with rubbing boys through their pants until they came. The grunts and groans that culminated in the wet spot that grew on the front of their Levi's gave her a sense of visceral relief and calm. It was as if she owned them. Next, Mira graduated to liberating their young shafts from their pants, watching them spring to life as she popped the button and unzipped the fly, pulling and rubbed them dispassionately until they came all over themselves, then carefully cleaning her hand directly on the front of their shirts. She giggled inside, wondering how they explained the stains to their friends and family members when they arrived home.

Mira and her girlfriends graduated to engaging in blowjob contests, comparing notes about giving the best one. Mira touted herself as an accomplished fellator and lied to her cohort that she could deep throat and swallow. But if she ever put her face near a boy's erection, it disgusted her. Nevertheless, her friends believed her stories and held her in what appeared to be reverence and high esteem.

Once she started allowing boys to enter her, it reduced the experience to a more tolerable level. She could close her eyes, lay her body back, and disassociate. Before any of their body parts became connected, she secretly moved up to the ceiling of the room, feeling nothing while waiting for the inevitable culmination of the act—the boy making his final few thrusts, vibrating on top of her while she remained anesthetized inside. She waited patiently outside her body for him to finish, his fluid invisibly injected into her without a trace—not seen, smelled, or felt—while her eyes remained closed, her face frozen in dispassion. Sometimes if he took too long, she panted rehearsed feline sounds of pleasure, finally screaming out a lustful mock orgasm to bring him off without delay. She quickly headed to the bathroom to wash the smell of sex from her body. Unknown to her, she left important parts of her soul on the ceilings of each of the rooms she occupied, those soul pieces remaining there for her to retrieve when she was ready.

"Hey, where did you go?" Spit asked. "You seemed to be in a trance there."

Startled back to consciousness, Mira replied, "I'm fine. Let's get the fuck out of here. Do you have somewhere we can party?"

| 29 |

Mira and Split walked the few blocks down First Avenue to the Show Box nightclub. On the way, Split pulled a joint out of his pocket, fired it up, and handed it over to Mira. She drew the familiar smoke deep into her. For a moment, she pondered how her ethereal being could smoke a joint while being disembodied. But, as the luscious euphoria of the drug seeped into her and her persistent internal dialogue relaxed, she let go of all extraneous thoughts. She offered the joint back to Split, not noticing he'd fired up one of his own. By the time they reached the Show Box, she was blissfully floating in a familiar fog of uncaring.

The place thumped and vibrated with the sound of loud mu.sic and people yelling at each other, trying to communicate over the din. As soon as she heard the raspy voice, the dark lyrics, and the painful sound, she knew the DJ was playing her kind of mu.sic. She made her way into the main showroom and looked up to see Kurt Cobain live on the stage, screaming out the words of Lithium to himself and the crowd:

I'm so lonely, but that's okay.
I shaved my head,

And I'm not sad.
And just maybe I'm to blame for all I've heard,
But I'm not sure.

Mira knew Kurt had blown his head off with a shotgun in 1994. She'd been too young to remember him alive, but came to appreciate his lyrics and sounds as a teenager. Perhaps she'd heard about his suicide but didn't understand what it meant. So she googled him after becoming entranced with his sounds:

On April 8, 1994, Kurt Cobain, the lead singer and guitarist of the grunge band Nirvana, was found dead at his home in Seattle, Washington. Forensic analysis at the time determined he had died by suicide three days earlier. The Seattle Police Department incident report states, "Kurt Cobain was found with a shotgun across his body, had a visible head wound, and there was a suicide note discovered nearby. In addition, the King County Medical Examiner noted puncture wounds on the inside of both the right and left elbow. Prior to his death, Cobain had checked out of a drug rehabilitation facility and had been reported as suicidal by his wife, Courtney Love."

Mira lost count of how many times she'd heard the song Lithium. She listened to it at raves, house parties, through the headphones of a CD player, high, straight, dancing, and fucking. But this time, the words seemed different, more personal.

Split's voice broke her trance. "Come with me . . . I want to show you something."

Split took Mira by the hand and led her out of

the showroom, down a back hallway away from the crowd and stage. They followed a dimly lit hallway to a series of numbered doors. Split stopped outside door number four, pulled a grimy key out of his frayed Levi's pocket, and slipped the key into the lock. Then, pushing through the door, he took Mira by the hand and led her into a windowless room, empty except for a small wooden table next to a stained, bare mattress on the floor. A single yellow light hung from the ceiling of the room.

He reached into the side pocket of his faded World War II army-fatigue jacket, pulled the contents out, and placed them on the wooden table. Then he stripped off his jacket and sat on the stained mattress. His fading-grey T-shirt bore a picture of John Lennon and the word *Imagine* printed across the chest. He grabbed Mira's hand and pulled her down beside him. He looked straight into her. "I know how you got here," he said. "You dumped an entire bottle of fentanyl down your throat before you even thought about it. I know how you felt. We're no different from each other."

Mira lowered her head. "I'd been thinking about it since I started high school and just couldn't tell anyone. I thought the feelings would go away on their own when I was older, but they just got worse. Everything was piling up, and I wanted out. I didn't expect it to happen the way it did. I just couldn't imagine going on the way I felt all the time. But I didn't expect this in-between place . . . nobody said you have to go through this . . . it sucks."

"Mine was a complete accident," Split explained. "I just liked to party a lot. At one crazy rave, someone slipped me some pills and said they were ecstasy. It turns out they were black-market fentanyl. I took a bunch, expecting a fun night, and then the lights went out. The next thing I know, I'm here, and everything is easy. I don't have to think about anything. You don't need money—nothing to buy—and nobody expects anything from you. I just float around chilling. So what do you mean by 'in-between place'? Nobody told me this was an in-between place."

"If you don't need money, why do you work at the coffee shop?"

"Work at the coffee shop? I don't work at a coffee shop. What gave you that idea?"

"What do you mean, you don't work at a coffee shop? I was just there, talking with my grandma, and you brought us tea and scones."

"That was your trip, not mine; I just got here," Split explained. "You make me into whatever you need to understand. Being here with me now . . . this is your trip, too. We're all just pure energy here. In this place, our energies mingle, and we create whatever visuals we need to process. Here, it's like virtual reality on steroids with no hardware needed."

"Jesus . . ." Mira muttered to herself.

"You can bring him around, too, if you like. Just call him up, and he'll come right over."

Mira let Split's comment pass.

"So this is all a hallucination?" Mira asked. "I read about death hallucinations—'the delusions of a dying brain,' they called it."

"Hallucinations? You need a brain and a mind to hallucinate," Split replied. "Your human body is no longer breathing. Your human body is flatlined back there in that expensive condo of yours. You're 'unresponsive' as they say . . . dead, croaked, morte. Those EMTs are artificially forcing air into your lungs and mas.saging your chest, forcing blood to circulate through your ves.sels. They're trying to keep your cells from dying while they try to resuscitate you. But your lungs don't work anymore, and your body can't sustain life on its own. You're dead, girl. Put that in your pipe and smoke it. This is as real as it gets. Here, there's no real and unreal, right and wrong, good and bad, up and down, true and false. Here . . ."

Split droned on, and Nona's words came back to Mira:

True.

Not true.

Not not true.

"Here, we appear to each other in ways we can understand. Otherwise, we can't change, can't learn, can't grow, can't move on," Split explained.

"Learn what? Move on to what?" Mira asked.

"Whatever we choose."

Mira's spirit whirled like a fidget spinner. She'd had enough. "I thought you brought me here to party?"

"It's your call, your trip. I brought some special stuff for you to try." Split turned to the small wooden table next to the mattress and placed on it a square of aluminum foil, a small translucent envelope containing a dirty white powder, a Zippo lighter, and a one cc syringe. Mira watched as he carefully folded a crease into the foil, lifted it between his first two fingers, picked up the envelope, and tapped the contents into the center of the foil. After dropping the empty envelope onto the table, he picked up his Zippo, deftly flicked it open with his thumb and forefinger, and stroked the flint wheel with his thumb, producing a perfect flame to heat the contents on the foil.

Within seconds, the powder turned to a clear liquid, and seconds beyond that, it bubbled with anticipation. Split flicked the cover of his Zippo closed and placed it and the foil onto the table, then he picked up the syringe and gave the plunger two quick pulls and pushes in and out before placing the point of the syringe into the liquid. He pulled about one-half cc into the barrel of the syringe, then lifted the tube in front of his eyes, flicked it twice with his finger, and pushed a few droplets of the precious liquid out of the tip of the needle.

Turning to Mira, he said, "Are you ready for the trip of your life?"

"Isn't it more like the trip of my death?" she quipped, holding out her right arm. "I've never injected before. What is that shit?"

"Let's say it's like nothing on earth." Split tied Mira off at the elbow and inserted the fluid into her. "Plus, there's no danger of overdose since our previous lives have already ended."

As he pushed the warm drug into Mira, an

ecstatic bliss came over her and embraced her. She swirled through the cosmos in complete rapture. Without a body, there were no physical sensations. She was free and unencumbered. Yet, as the sensations overtook her, unanswered questions swirled around her. Who is Nona really, and what was she trying to teach me? I know she isn't my real Nona, so why was she here? And what's the real meaning of true, not true, and not not true? I want to understand . . . I want to understand . . . Help me understand.

Kaleidoscopes of vivid colors swirled around her as her queries quieted. New and vibrant hues wove into her. Braids of blood-red, bright orange, golden yellow, emerald green, navy blue, sparkling violet, and blazing pearl white surrounded her, immersing her in a beauty previously unknown to her. Divine feminine energy embraced her, and she bathed in it. Finally, she was ready to move forward. She felt complete with what she'd intended to finish here. The total peace she'd wished for now enveloped her, save for one minor detail that remained—Split.

As if right on cue, there he was, standing stark naked before her. "Now, let's really get this party started!" He stepped in front of her, ready to place a rock-hard shaft directly onto Mira's spiritual lips.

In her state of intoxicated bliss, Mira became confused. Had she been in the physical body she'd just left, she would've given Split the blow job of his life, gotten it over with, and felt that old familiar power. Then, extreme loneliness and shame would follow. She paused for a moment and looked up into Split's face. It slowly became the face of the fourteen-year-old boy at the house party, and then the face of Ian, and then the face of Sergei, and then the face of everyone she'd had sex with when she was too young, or too vulnerable, or too high, or blacked out. Instead of robotically complying, she allowed a feeling she'd never acknowledged or indulged to arise in her. She was livid. Enraged. Furious.

What was he thinking? That her purpose was to service him without consideration? Who did he think he was? An entitled, self-indulgent man-child with no sense of decency and care? That he had permission to take what he wanted when he wanted it? That his needs were more important than hers? Could he not see that she was a separate person from him with feelings and needs of her own? Her undeniable rage, erupting for the first time, became overwhelming and uncontainable. If Split had been in human form, she might've torn him apart, limb from limb.

Then she remembered Split's story about how he got his name from the shrink who came into the coffee shop. He called him "Split" and suggested he look up the meaning but Split never did. So what did he want Split to understand?

Mira recalled Nona's words and the words of her own wise woman as they came back to her into sharp focus. Mira finally understood what was not not true: that she was Split, and Split was her. Split existed as her own darkness. He existed as her depression, her isolation, her self-loathing, her addiction, her suicide.

Everything that was not not true fell into place;

that she was Nona, and Nona was her; that she was Martin, and Martin was her; that she was Gina, and Gina was her; that her ancestors were her, and she was her ancestors. And yes, she was Sergei, and Sergei was her. So she finally understood that life was death, and death was life. It was all that she made it to be. It was all true, and it was all not true, and it was all not not true. And now she knew what she felt, and she knew what to do.

Mira put a bookmark on her rage, knowing she had a job to finish first. Then, calling upon all the spirits of the Mystery to support her, she firmly pushed Split from in front of her, sat him down on the stained mattress, and lovingly swaddled his naked being in a soft blanket, as she would've wrapped a newborn baby. She folded her arms around his fragile spirit and spoke to him in a soft and reassuring tone.

"You've stayed here too long. This is not a place in which to remain. Treat it as a stopping-off place, an in-between place. It's a place for you to reflect, to heal, and to purify. You have interrupted your natural cycle by staying here, and, as long as you're here, I'll stay here to care for you. I know now that I'm here to help you move on. You lost your connection to the Mystery beyond all Mysteries. You lost track of your connection to the divine. But, by attaching your spirit to my spirit, you're contaminating me by staying here, and now I'm contaminating you. It's time for both of us to move on from each other."

Split bore a confused look of acceptance. His energy softened and relaxed.

"It's time for you to move into and join the light. I have some business to finish, but I promise to follow when I'm ready. You'll be safe moving on; you know you can trust the light that will come to you."

As Mira spoke, a brilliant column of light descended onto Split's energy field. He started vibrating at a frequency he'd never experienced and began separating from Mira and moving up into the column of light. As Split rose into the sparkling silver-white light, he never looked back. Mira felt a deep sense of grief as Split departed as if a part of her went with him. They'd traveled the millennia together, but now was time for new beginnings. Her deep sorrow soon turned to relief and excitement. She felt complete, ready to continue her journey.

~

While darkness enveloped the Seattle sky outside the condo, Marty continued to push air into the lifeless body lying prone on the gurney. Finally, he solemnly stood before her, his eyes softly closed and head bowed as if in silent prayer before a sacred altar. After a while, he opened his eyes, preparing to utter his well-rehearsed time-of-death declaration.

"Hold on, Marty," his partner murmured. "I've got a faint heartbeat."

Marty held his breath, waiting. "It seems a little stronger, but she's still not breathing on her own. Do you want to try transporting?"

"Let's wait to see if we get a normal EKG. If we can get that, we can transport while she's still intubated."

| 30 |

Mira rested comfortably lying in the lush grasses of the Serengeti savannah on the African continent. Hundreds of white-bearded wildebeest and zebra grazed peacefully with each other as warm moist breezes rustled through the tall grasses. During her embodied life, she wanted to visit the region, and now she had the time and space to do so. Like the fresh mint she infused into her tea every morning, her recent experiences continued to integrate into her spirit. So she hadn't noticed the presence that joined her while she enjoyed her personal safari.

"Wow, what you did with Split was amazing. Thanks for including me."

Mira turned to the left and found herself face-to-face with an enormous grey-brown she-elephant. She felt a quiet power emanating from the grand being unlike any she'd felt before. "Okay, Nona, I get it. What's not not true, is that I am the elephant, and the elephant is me; I get it." Mira chuckled.

"It was as if you'd tied yourself to him like a sailboat tethered to a dock. You had to loosen the line if you were ever to go sailing. Releasing him to the light was brilliant," the elephant said, winking at her own pun. "Perhaps you can use the rage you felt when he expected you to pleasure him with no consideration or acknowledgment of you."

"Use the rage? What do you mean? Rage is rage. Humans express rage with violence and destruction."

"Like the rage Sergei showed when he raped you as a small child?"

"That wasn't rage. He was taking sex with no regard for me at all."

"Really? Think about it . . . he was getting sex from Gina—all he wanted and every type. She never turned him down. His rage with women and an insatiable need for control and power motivated him to attack you in his blind stupor. The sex Sergei got from Gina and all the women before Gina didn't satisfy what was boiling inside of him from long ago. Then, when Split pushed sex on you a while ago, your natural reactions came up. You knew he wasn't interested in lovingly connecting with you but only wanted to relieve his unquenchable thirst for power and control."

"He was so transparent and pathetic, and I felt sorry for him. I could tell how insecure he was inside and how having sex with me would make him feel better about himself. I think I've done that . . . had sex with men to feel like I was worthy of someone's attention. But, unfortunately, it never made me feel better."

"But, this time, instead of catering to his needs because you could relate to his feelings of insecurity, you let your own need for healthy power and control to emerge. You felt your anger about what he was doing and used it to separate your energy from his. In fact, once you used your anger to create safety for yourself by setting clear and firm boundaries, you treated him with love and concern and sent him on his way."

"I felt a little guilty doing that, but I knew I would feel worse if I gave in."

"Back when you were so small, when Sergei attacked you in what you thought was the safety of your room and your bed, and no one was there to protect you, you were too powerless and unknowing to realize that the first thing you needed was to get yourself to safety, no matter what it took. So you froze, which is understandable for a seven-year-old, especially one who'd lost her father."

"What else could I have done? He was an adult, and I was just a kid. And he was mom's boyfriend."

"That's what your head told you. But you could have let your body decide what you needed and let your natural physical and emotional instincts for protection and safety come forward. You might have been able to let your body take over and free it to respond in any way it saw fit. So, if you like, we could go back there together and let your body react the way it wanted to when fueled by the natural anger you experienced under attack."

"I don't know what you're talking about. They never allowed me to show my anger when I was young. If I yelled or slammed a door, Mom yelled louder and sent me to my room. If I kicked or threw something, she smacked my butt until I cried."

"So every time you felt or expressed anger, they punished you with restrictions or physical pain. That drove your natural physical expression of anger inwards. It might have been better if your mom had taught you to release your physical anger in healthy ways, like screaming into a pillow or punching a punching bag."

The gentle she-elephant continued without pausing, "So here's an important clue about how to understand anger: anger is the energy that drives champions. People who achieve amazing feats know how to mobilize their anger into power, drive, persistence, and stamina. Think of your heroes. Remember the video of Brandi Chastain kicking the winning world-cup goal in the 1999 Olympic Games? She ran across the field, sliding to her knees, ripped off her jersey to show her chiseled torso to the world, raised her clenched fists to the sky, and screamed out in triumph. For weeks, sportscasters debated whether she was 'unladylike' even though her sports bra fully covered her chest.

"Or the time Serena Williams lost her cool and called a chair umpire a 'liar and a thief' for penalizing her in a finals match that cost her the crown. Officials tolerated that kind of behavior from John McEnroe for years without penalty. Those women learned to turn their anger into power, just like their male counterparts. You never expressed your anger as a child, so you didn't learn how to channel it into your power. What child molesters count on most is the powerlessness of children. They know children are unlikely to protect themselves and unlikely to report what happened to them. Children are more likely to blame themselves and feel shame. What might have happened if you'd engaged your natural power, your anger, when Sergei attacked you? As an experiment, would you like to see, to feel how it might have been? To experience the same incident if you used your anger and engaged your physical, emotional, and mental power? What do you have to lose?"

Mira froze for a moment, listening to the elephant's graphic images. "I don't know if I can do it. Can I bear to go through that again? Do I have what it takes? I'm afraid it will happen again just as it did the first time, only this time it will be worse knowing what's coming."

"You won't be going through it again; you'll go through it differently. We both know it happened just the way it did the first time, so there'll be no surprise. Only this time, it'll be a redo, an opportunity for you to experience it from a higher plane and perhaps even correct what happened to you. I'll be there, too, and Nona, and Martin, along with all the other little girls who experienced the same trauma as you."

The great elephant's last pronouncement brought Mira up short. "All the other little girls? All the other little girls!" The words pierced Mira's open-hearted spirit as she imagined all the other little girls who'd suffered sexual and physical abuse as she had. And, as she did, blind rage boiled up inside of her like Mount Saint Helens just before she blew her top.

Suddenly the putrid smell was back in her nose.

The disgusting taste was back in her mouth. She started gagging and choking, and her entire little body stiffened in shock and fear. Then, again she forced herself to open her eyes and saw the bright orange-red flame ignite the center of Sergei's eyeballs. But now, as Mira looked just beyond those hideous devil-eyes, her gaze fell on the powerful big brown eyes of her elephant peering down from the ceiling. And she saw standing behind the elephant, all of her ancestors—her grandfathers and grandmothers; her great-grandfathers and great-grandmothers—all the way back seven generations.

And this time, the flash of evil orange-red light in Sergei's eyes ignited a reservoir of righteous anger lying dormant in Mira's ancient soul and the souls of Rose and Miriam and Barak. It lit the rage of her entire tribe who'd perished in the death chambers of the Holocaust, and all her ancestors stolen from their families in Africa and sold into slavery. Without knowing how she knew, she channeled her sea of anger and called upon the spirits of Nemesis, the Goddess of Indignation and Retribution; Athena, the Goddess of Wisdom, Courage, and Justice; and Kali, the Slayer of Ego and Liberator of the Soul, to be with her and to empower her.

And then little Mira, with the might and fury of the Goddess warriors of the ages mobilized to empower her, tightened every muscle in her body, twisted and turned, pushed and punched, kicked and kneed, pulling her head violently from side to side until she freed her face and body from under Sergei's weight and power. And as she pulled herself free from his grasp, Mira's face lifted to the heavens, and her throat erupted in a mighty banshee scream that pushed to the far reaches of the universe. And finally, she jumped from her bed and bolted from the room with all of her innocence intact.

| 31 |

"Liebe, I must show you something. There's something you must see."

"You're back! Where did you go? I missed you."

"I had a mission to complete, Liebe. You'll know about that later. But now I am back, and you must see what I have to show you. You need to see this."

~

Under blue Seattle skies, a young woman jogged along Lake Washington Boulevard, warmed by the summer sun. Hydro-gen-powered Hoverpods, pregnant with standing passengers, floated peacefully over the boulevard. They had replaced gas-and electric-powered automobiles after the government banned them from the Seattle streets years ago. Millions of tiny, biodegradable air scrubbers no bigger than gnats flew high over Lake Washington. They sequestered airborne carbon for recycling and spilled clean air back into the atmosphere before falling and dissolving into the water, quickly replaced by new ones.

Fresh, clean air flowed easily in and out of her lungs, her breathing maintaining a metronome cadence in time with the clap of her feet on the surface of the running path. She inhaled to the count of five and exhaled to the count of five, feeling the oxygen molecules as they entered her cells and carbon dioxide molecules as they left. She floated in the deep satisfaction of the rhythm of her body and the bliss of her runner's high. Mira's spirit jogged along with her, joined by a separate but strangely familiar spirit.

"Is that me?" Mira asked.

"Well, no, Liebe, not quite. Perhaps partly, but not quite."

Not not true, Mira thought.

The hot pink of the cherry blossoms exploded on the brilliant background of the deep-blue Seattle sky. Bright sunlight mirrored from millions of petals illuminated the young woman's skin with an indelible glow of golden pink that reflected skyward to the outer reaches of the universe. Yet, she was oblivious to the tiny clump of cells growing in the folds of her uterus.

Weeks later, the young woman sensed that another presence had joined her—another being housed in the confines of her body. It confused her at first, and she dismissed the sensations as meaningless.

Later, the obvious emerged. "I missed my period this month," she tentatively informed her partner. "Probably just stress."

He felt the birth of excitement along with gripping fear deep in his gut but dismissed the sensations as symptoms of indigestion. "That's weird. Are you feeling anything else?"

"Just a little tired and nauseous."

The home pregnancy test returned a positive result. They'd only been together for the past year, and she was planning to take her graduate records exam in just a few weeks to apply for a master's program. It wasn't the time to be pregnant. But the being who tumbled from the cosmos into the clump of cells growing inside her proved to be powerful and undeniable. They'd known each other before and would know each other again. This being had lived many cycles and possessed a clear mission and intention for this new iteration.

"I'm pregnant!" the woman informed her partner.

His shock left him speechless.

~

Mira tried to understand the information download. "Now I know for a fact that cannot be me. I would never have a baby—too much trouble."

"I already said you're not that woman, Liebe," her companion said. Not not true.

~

With her cell phone in hand, the young woman cried outside an abortion clinic. "But what about grad school, Mom? Brad just got a good job, and the student loans would kill us if I can't go to work right after school. And, with Dad gone, we need to think about taking care of you, too."

"It's your choice, dear one," her mom replied, "but we can work it out if you want to have the baby. You're not to worry about me; that's not your place! Anyway, this is amazing! What did Brad say?"

"He said the same thing, 'we'll work it out whatever I decide.' But whenever I talk about having an abortion, his eyes well up with tears. He told me he always saw us having children and can't wait to see what we get."

A few minutes later, the young woman stepped onto a Hoverpod, and a new adventure began.

~

Mira struggled to integrate the information. "Okay, it all made sense until now, but who the hell are these people? I don't recognize anyone here, and I sure as hell don't know what's going on."

"Think about it, Liebe. What's not not true here; if you're not the young woman, and you are not her partner, Brad, and you're not her mother . . ."

"Oh, shit!" Mira exclaimed.

"I'm not ready for this yet! Take me back now! I get it! I get it! That's too freaky! I'm ready to go back. I'm not ready to move on! Take me back now."

| 32 |

Mira rubbed the sleep from her eyes as she slowly returned to wakefulness. She looked around her condo, trying to orient herself. Her memories of last night were hazy and jumbled. She looked down and saw she still wore the same clothes she'd worn on her ride back from Portland. She must have passed out sitting in her living room recliner again. It wasn't the first time she'd done so.

Mira struggled to piece together the details of her return home. She remembered the train ride from Portland to Seattle and taking oxys and fentanyl the entire way back to calm her raw emotions. But she didn't remember coming through her door or how she ended up spending the night in her recliner.

The sharp whistle of her automatic teapot in the kitchen interrupted her thoughts. Had she programmed it to brew last night before collapsing in her chair? Her memory flashed to holding her father's lifeless hand, and then the numb train ride back—nothing after that.

Mira turned to look down at the surface of the side table next to her chair. Shreds of a torn-up letter and envelope lay scattered there with its pieces small and unreadable. She picked up and smoothed out one marked piece. When she saw the name Ian signed on the shard of paper, the contents of the letter returned to her:

I'm sorry I left in such a crappy way, but it is what it is. I wish you all the luck in the world. Sorry about your dad. Ian.

An acrid metal taste crept into her mouth. Her recollection grew clearer.

Mira stood and took a step toward the kitchen to turn off the shrieking teapot. "Shit!" she cried. A blunt object intruded deep into her instep. "Shit!"

She reached down and picked up the offending article—a prescription bottle cap. Just under the coffee table, a foot or two away, she spied the empty pill bottle to which the cap belonged. She reached around the table leg, picked the container off the carpet, and held it up in front of her eyes. Fentanyl. As Mira read her name printed on the label, a dreamy image of a young woman throwing her head back and emptying the entire contents of small white pills into her mouth passed through her memory like a poorly written scene from a B-grade Netflix movie. She watched the young woman slump into her chair as her breathing slowed and finally stopped.

Mira sat back onto her chair and closed her eyes as the full memory of her overdose downloaded into her conscious awareness: her travels with the spirit of Jakob who called her Liebe and accompanied her to keep her safe; her visits with Nona Rose and her encounters with her past lives to recover lost parts of her soul; the she-elephant who helped her become a teacher herself; and the return of her Lieber spirit guide to give her a glimpse of her future life. Had she been alive or dead? Could it all have been a hallucination? Was she in her body or somewhere else? What was she to believe?

With a start, she remembered the paramedics in her house. She seemed to return to consciousness once or twice after she'd overdosed—or had she? A man and a woman had been trying to save her. He was an African-American man with skin the color of her father's. She even remembered the man's name from his name tag—Martin, just like her father. They'd given her Narcan and resuscitated her, hadn't they?.

So if paramedics came, she must have overdosed and stopped breathing. She must have been dead for a time and had the type of death hallucinations she'd read about. But how did the paramedics know to come? Who had called them? Ian had left her.

Her watch! It must have been her watch. Mira reached down and felt for her Smart Watch strapped to her wrist. It had an emergency SOS feature that dialed 911 if it detected that the wearer fell or if their pulse stopped. It must have detected that her heart stopped and called 911 automatically. The medics must have come, and building security must have admitted them. Then they must have left once she was stable.

Mira checked the call history on her watch and phone—no calls to 911. She opened her computer and checked the security log on her front door—it had logged no entries after she returned last night, and no log existed of anyone leaving. She saw no physical evidence of anyone being in her house during the night—no medical packaging or leftovers. And if the paramedics had resuscitated her from an overdose, wouldn't they have transported her to the hospital for treatment and observation? She would've had to talk with a psychiatrist before being discharged. They'd never have left her alone in her home after taking an overdose.

As Mira continued to question if her experiences during the night were real—true or not true, she heard Nona Rose's words come to her loud and clear: her experience was not not true, something she'd never experienced before.

On her way through the kitchen, Mira threw the bottle and its cap into the garbage can and decided she would answer all the questions she had in the days to follow. She brewed a cup of tea for herself and thought about the people in her life who were no longer with her: Nona and Martin. She thought about all the close friends she'd made in grade school and high school and all the people she went to college with. And then she flashed back to hearing Louis Armstrong singing out of her grandmother's phonograph. She sang along with the lyrics she heard in her head:

I see friends shaking hands,
Saying, 'How do you do?'
They're really saying,
'I love you.'

Mira returned to her chair to enjoy her tea. Her

mental and visual acuity seemed sharper than ever this morning. The view from her window was clearer and brighter and more alive than ever. She felt as if she'd awakened from a deep and satisfying sleep, greater than any she'd previously experienced, and she greeted this day as if she'd just been born. Mira felt a peace she'd never felt before—and yet one she'd known all along.

She sat in the morning light that streamed through the tall windows. Puget Sound glistened with diamond-sharp sparkles.

The Olympic Mountains and Hurricane Ridge peaks still wore a shower cap of last winter's snow. The eastbound ferry from Bremerton to Seattle weaved a lazy wake behind its green and white hull as it steamed across Puget Sound, destined for Pier 52 with its cargo of early morning commuters.

Mira turned her gaze to the north and caught the last cruise ship of the season leaving Pier 91. It would repeat its voyage northward through Alaska's Inside Passage to treat her passengers to the astonishing scenes of Canada and Alaska.

Mira looked at the bare walls of her condo; they felt cold and wanting. Gina had carefully put away all the picture albums from Mira's childhood, thinking they would upset her. Now she knew that their absence upset her more, so she found a place on the wall to plan for a photo gallery of her loved ones.

It was time for her to celebrate her childhood and honor the people who'd brought her into the world. She wanted to remember all the people she'd met and gotten to know as friends. But, she realized she hadn't learned how to care about people and how to let them care about her.

While she stood at her kitchen counter buttering a slice of toast to go with her tea, Mira found herself transported back to a scene from her past. She became a ten-year-old girl standing in the kitchen of her best friend, Rebecca's, house.

She remembered Rebecca's grandfather making sandwiches for lunch. He held a butter knife and spread thick peanut butter and fragrant grape jelly onto dark-brown rye toast, placing the finished product on plates next to tall glasses of cold milk. Mira's gaze fell on the six faded-blue numbers etched permanently into the skin of his left forearm.

Then, compelled by influences she didn't understand, Mira asked Rebecca's grandfather, "Do you know why you are here? I don't know why I'm here or even why any of us are here. We all seem to do the same thing every day. We go to school, and our parents work and worry about making enough money. They worry about what other people think of us or are doing to us. So why are we all here?"

She recalled how Rebecca's grandfather stopped what he was doing, leaned over to Mira, locked his dark-brown eyes onto hers, and replied in his thick European accent, "You have just asked the most important question of your young life. Finding your life's purpose is exactly why you're here. It's taken me a very long time and a lot of soul searching to find my purpose. But, in my life, I am very clear why I'm here.

Would you like to know?"

She nodded in anticipation.

Then, she remembered how Rebecca's grandfather pulled himself up tall and stated proudly, "The reason I'm here is to love and be loved unconditionally. To do that, I must love myself unconditionally. That means I must love myself without question, without doubt, without pause. I'm still learning how to love myself unconditionally, but I'm getting better at it every day. So, if you like, you may borrow my life's purpose for yourself until you find a better one. I've found no better one yet."

After Mira returned from her childhood memory, she repeated Nona Rose's words to herself: not not true.

Could it be that simple? Wasn't she supposed to find a husband, settle down, have children, get degrees, find better jobs, make a lot of money, and buy houses and cars? Or could it be that the purpose for her life was the same as it was for Rebecca's grandfather? On this special morning, Mira decided it was the best purpose she could ever choose.

So she returned to the kitchen, scooped a teaspoon of her favorite Genmaicha green tea into a fabric tea bag, and tied it off at the top. She placed it in her favorite porcelain mug and added scalding water from her still-boiling teapot. While making her way back into the living room, she imagined the touch of her Nona's fingers as she fashioned Mira's crimson hair into two perfect braids while they listened to her scratchy phonograph. She sorely missed her Nona's loving touch.

"Hey, Google, play Louie Armstrong's What a Wonderful World," Mira called out as if she were with an old friend. She sat back down in her recliner with her tea and toast, took a deep breath, slowly let it out, and sang along in harmony with Louie's raspy voice:

I hear babies cry;
I watch them grow;
They'll learn much more
Then I'll ever know,
And I think to myself,
What a wonderful world.
Yes, I think to myself.
What a wonderful world.

| 33 |

In the following weeks, months, and years, Mira worked to integrate her experience. She sought theological, scientific, and para-scientific answers to the questions it posed, so she took up the study of comparative religions, metaphysics, and quantum physics. In addition, she studied Judaism, Hinduism, Buddhism, Islam, and the beliefs of the First Nation Tribes of North America. Since Gina had raised her in the teachings of the Roman Catholic Church, Mira had celebrated the major Christian holidays every year as a matter of rote habit. Still, she never felt emotionally moved by Christianity, and she even told her friends she never bought into the "Jesus son of God thing." She knew that no single religion could meet her spiritual needs but longed to find a community to support her growing beliefs and values.

As Mira expanded her reading and study and realized she'd used drugs as an anesthetic for her deeper understanding of herself and the universe, she reached into the twelve-step recovery community for support. There she developed a deeper understanding of the connections between her addiction, losing her spiritual connection, and the danger of family secrets.

Her studies led her to conclude that while one belief system could never serve all her spiritual needs, many could inform her. So she applied the teachings of true, not true, and not not true to her studies and came to believe everything she learned and nothing she learned at the same time. As a result, She tried to begin each day with an empty and unknowing mind.

In her studies, she came upon the stories and aspects of the Archangel Michael. Knowing that he represented a character in a story—an archetype, she came to feel his strength and courage and called on him to help her overcome her fears. She loved that Michael appeared in the Book of Daniel of the Hebrew Bible, the Book of Revelations of the Christian Bible, and again in the Quran of the Muslim faith. Throughout the years that followed her overdose, she searched for an explanation for the healing teachings she'd received during her time with her spirit guides. Was it Michael's protective presence accompanying her on her journey into death and his voice that guided her on her quest to find the purpose for her life? Was it Martin's, or perhaps the collection of her ancestors —Nona, Miriam, Barak? Martin's grandmother Duba? Was it all of them together, or perhaps none of them at all? She loved living in the paradox of not not true to answer the questions she posed, accepting that it was all part of the Great Mystery and that she could play in it like a child in her sandbox with the best toys ever.

Because of the abuses of authority and spiritual injuries that she bore, Mira struggled with the concept of God. The Catholic teachings that Gina and the church offered meant nothing real to her, and she'd abandoned those ideas long ago. But she knew the mysterious energies she encountered during her death were more powerful than any on earth—energies that possessed great strength and even greater love. She embraced the Mystery beyond all Mysteries, and that concept brought her peace. She needed no further explanation. The archetype of Archangel Michael embodied the Mystery beyond all Mysteries. It explained the presence she felt after returning from her journey.

She married her first husband, Justin, a few years later—a somewhat geeky, nondescript computer engineer. After they had two children, they joined a spiritual community in Seattle that presented itself as nondenominational so their children could have a spiritual experience. She attended services and lectures there, and while she liked the people she met and the messages of love and kindness, it felt like spiritual-lite to her. The kids enjoyed playing with the other kids, but that's all they were doing: playing. She felt uncomfortable when the community celebrated Christian holidays, including Christmas and Easter, referring to them as nondenominational.

"Doesn't Christmas celebrate the birth of Jesus Christ?" she queried without answer.

After a few years, dissatisfied with her religious community and her husband, Mira left them both to raise her children as a single parent. She still longed for a community that fit her and her children. Her seeking brought her back to her computer to search the historical archives. She already knew the names of her German Jewish and Italian Jewish ancestors, and the Holocaust historians kept meticulous archives of the families lost in Hitler's gas chambers. The Nazis were also meticulous record keepers with their system of tattooing identification numbers on their victims' forearms. It didn't take long for her to find the fates of both sides of Rose's extended family. She knew the Nazis executed Rose's father and grandparents outside their home, and she found that all other members of her family had perished in the gas chambers of Auschwitz. She found no trace of Barak's extended family and assumed they had perished as well. After Miriam passed in New York, Rose became an orphan forever, separating Mira from her extended family.

While Mira grieved the loss of her direct blood-lines, she decided the Nazis could never exterminate Judaism, just as all the others who had tried and failed to do so through the ages. She knew that Judaism still lived within her; no one could deny her that fact. While she couldn't fathom a "Jewish God," she knew what was not not true; that she was a part of the Jewish people by ancestry, and she also belonged to the Mystery beyond all Mysteries, just as all people do.

One day, on an impulse, Mira visited a Friday night Shabbat service in a small meditative synagogue on Capitol Hill. She'd heard about the congregation from a friend she'd met in her twelve-step recovery program. A nontraditional rabbi and psychologist who followed the meditative practices of the Hindu gurus had founded it years ago. The synagogue shared space in a beautiful Baptist church with a towering bell tower. Every other Friday night, the congregants transformed the church's altar into the synagogue's bimah for their Shabbat services.

Mira slipped into the sanctuary and sat alone in a pew near the back of the gathering, trying her best to remain unnoticed. She picked up a prayer book on her way in and read along as everyone recited the prayers in Hebrew and English while she kept her coat on and her purse in her lap. She found the words comforting and relaxing, as most were simple words of praise for the divine.

Near the middle of the service, the Rabbi asked everyone to take their seats and quietly intoned, "As I ask to bring down the lights in the sanctuary, let yourself close your eyes and find your breath." Mira looked around and saw everyone putting down their prayer books and closing their eyes. She tentatively closed her eyes and focused on the rise and fall of her chest, noticing all the tension in her body.

"Just listen to what I'm saying for the next few minutes and let yourself relax."

She waited for his next words.

"I'm inviting you to enter the energy of the Shabbat, of the Sabbath, the Day of Rest. So let yourself settle into your seat and drop down out of your head."

Mira focused on her breath.

"Relax your eyes . . .

And relax your neck . . .

And relax your chest . . .

and relax your belly." the Rabbi continued.

"We spend so much time worrying about little things. . . . For our time together this evening, let all the little things you worry about dissolve into thin air. Let yourself enter Shabbat consciousness and let yourself remain in Shabbat consciousness for the rest of Shabbat."

The rabbi spoke a while longer, but Mira was already floating on air, and his words didn't seem to matter. Then, before she knew it, she heard the words, "As the lights of the sanctuary come back up, you wake up fully relaxed and filled with the energy of Shabbat."

Mira enjoyed the gathering following the service with blessings over wine, bread, and some tasty treats and conversation. Then, the members convinced Mira to return the following morning to attend a Torah service, where the Rabbi would share his special story about the origins of the synagogue's Torah. Eager for more, she agreed.

The following day, Mira sat with the congregation for Shabbat morning services. When it came time to take the Torah out of its resting place to prepare to read the week's Torah portion, they opened the doors of the ark for everyone to see. The cantor sang special blessings for the beginning of the Torah service, and the Rabbi retrieved the small scroll from the hand-carved ark at the center of the bimah. Then, he turned back to the congregation and began the story of the history of the Torah he loved to repeat—and the gathering loved to hear:

"One day, in the middle of the seventeenth

century, somewhere in the Czech lands of the Holy Roman Empire, a Jewish scribe called a sofer rose early in the morning and went to the mikveh, the sacred bath, with a special purpose in mind. After purifying himself, submerged in the holy waters, he recited a heartfelt prayer of sacred intention. Then he selected a clean sheet of kosher parchment, dipped a feathered quill into a small pot of specially formulated ink, and wrote the first word of a new Torah scroll.

"B'reishit," he inscribed: "In the beginning."

The rabbi continued the tale he knew by heart. "He was scribing a small Torah, a Torah that a traveling rabbi would use to visit small congregations around the countryside, rather than a large scroll that would permanently stay within the ark of a home synagogue.

"Copying precisely from an existing text called a Tikkun—not daring to write from memory, even though he knew the entire Torah by heart, the scribe labored many hours a day, pausing only for midday prayers. He selected a special quill when the text called for him to write the holy name of God. He used the four Hebrew consonants YHVH, Yud, Hey, Vuv, Hey, so the reader would not utter the name of God aloud. Later, those letters morphed into the word Yahweh. After many months of painstaking work, the sofer inscribed the last words of the Torah: 'Never again did there arise in Israel a prophet like Moses, whom the Eternal singled out, face to face.'"

The rabbi went on with his teaching: "Once completed, our little Torah made its way to a synagogue in a small town in Czechoslovakia, not intended for one of the major synagogues in Prague, but most likely a synagogue similar to our own congregation here in Seattle. The town had suffered badly during the religious wars of earlier times—from the 1400s through the 1600s—and there was little room in Czech hearts for the Jews with their strange ways and beliefs. But, over time, the Jewish population increased in number, and their situation improved. By the mid-nineteenth century, there were perhaps fifty Jewish families in the little town and neighboring villages, enough to build a handsome synagogue with a school for the children."

The Rabbi paused, and his eyes sought the floor. "And then came the occupation by the Nazis, and all would change. First to suffer under the occupation were the Jews. The Nazis stripped them of their homes, their livelihoods, and all their human rights. In every city and village, including the little town, they rounded up the Jews and sent them first to a ghetto, and ultimately 'to the east,' as they called it, to the concentration camp called Auschwitz in Poland. They vandalized their synagogues, stole their gold and silver ornaments for their value, and destroyed their priceless Torah scrolls in their sudden attacks of hatred against the Jews.

To save what they could of their precious heritage, a few dedicated Jews in Prague gathered religious objects from all over Bohemia and Moravia, including our little Torah, and brought them to Prague for safekeeping. They established the Central Jewish Museum in Prague—not a Nazi creation, but a Jewish institution. Jewish leaders hoped the museum would be the safest place to store synagogue treasures until the war was over.

Through the secretive channels of collectors who specialize in antiquities, a London art dealer learned that the scrolls were for sale. Immediately, he put together a team: a generous donor who agreed to buy and donate the scrolls, a specialist who inspected the scrolls in Prague, and a rabbi who provided critical guidance about what they should do with the scrolls. The Czech Memorial Scrolls Trust was thus born. That organization of British Jews rescued 1,564 scrolls from a decaying warehouse in Prague and brought them to Westminster Synagogue in London. The year was 1964.

Some scrolls were so badly damaged—torn, burnt, and stained with blood—that they were no longer kosher, so they retired them. Sofers carefully restored the others and offered them on permanent loan to synagogues that could provide them with a loving home. Some went to synagogues, where they received status as Shoah survivors, preserved in special display cases as symbols of the past, but no longer functioning as active Torahs. Some shared space with other scrolls in a community's Aron ha-Kodesh only brought out for special occasions."

The Rabbi paused for a moment, cleared his throat, and collected himself. He seemed to hold the bundle in his arms tighter. "Little scroll #364 is one of the lucky ones that got a second chance at a joyful life.

She lives here in our community, which reveres her as a survivor and also chants her words and celebrates her presence by dancing in circles—a celebration that includes not only men, as in the old country, but now also women and children. That happy second life began when they entrusted her to our grateful community in 1993."

By now, as always, the young Rabbi's eyes filled with tears along with most of the gathering. Mira joined in with the rest. She felt her ancestors lost in the Holocaust there in the room with her. And she understood what was not not true about the events that befell her family so long ago in Cologne, Germany; that out of the seemingly insurmountable trauma of the genocide of the Jewish people at the hands of the Nazis arose a spiritual connection to YHVH that would endure forever. And that her connection would endure forever as well.

When he finished his story, the Rabbi handed the Torah to an official of the congregation, and, while everyone sang a special song and clapped together, they paraded the Torah around the sanctuary's aisles. As the Torah passed by, everyone pressed toward the aisle, holding out their prayer shawl or their prayer book to touch the Torah. Then they kissed the spot that had touched the Torah as if they'd kissed the holy book itself. When Mira touched her prayer book to the Torah and then touched the spot to her lips, she felt the piercing energy of 400 years of European Jewish antiquity flash through her. It seemed impossible and magical at the same time. Her cells vibrated. She knew she had returned to her family.

Mira felt a kinship with that little Torah. It was small, like her, and when the rabbi talked about the Torah, he referred to it in the feminine; it was "her" and "she." Mira felt like her childhood had been a bit of a Holocaust, one she'd survived. Perhaps they rescued her, or she saved herself, or maybe both. Ultimately, she reached her promised land, where she could live her purpose: to love herself unconditionally and to love and be loved by others unconditionally.

She thought about Nona Rose, Miriam, and Barak. Like the Israelites and their exodus from Egypt, they liberated themselves from oppression and received the blessings of deliverance to a promised land. She'd almost squandered the opportunity her ancestors gave to her. The Mystery beyond all Mysteries provided Mira with her second chance, just as it had the little Torah. On that day, when she first heard the story of the little Torah, Mira promised to honor her second life just as the congregation honored the little Torah's second life. She promised to live her purpose.

EPILOGUE

Mira lived well into her eighties. The years brought her the blessings and curses of not one but two more husbands who preceded her in death, along with three children and seven grandchildren, filling the balance of her years with joy and grief, stress and calm, before she peacefully departed the planet, surrounded in love. In her 90th year, Mira came to the time of her return to the Mystery in a place of peace with death. Her travels during her overdose and her adventures in the inter-life removed any fear or confusion she had about dying.

As she began her transition, Mira lay in her bed surrounded by her children and grandchildren. Deva Premal softly intoned the Hindu Gayatri mantra from a small speaker sitting on the bookcase. Members of her family softly kissed her forehead and laid their hands on her body. The images tattooed on the thin skin of her left arm she'd proudly worn throughout her life had faded. Her granddaughter had faithfully braided her once brilliant red hair, now smattered and streaked with grey, and laid the precise weave curled on the white pillow on which her head rested.

Everyone knew her time had come. Her breathing became slow and barely noticeable. Her eyes fluttered and closed. A final shallow breath entered Mira's lungs, only to remain unbreathed.

And then all was still. . .All was still.

Mira's spirit gently separated from her frail body and arose. Unseen by those around her, a column of super-brilliant, purple-white light descended over her, and she ascended into it. Mira looked down from above over those gathered around her, and a sublime peace came over her. As she continued her ascent, Mira blessed her family and friends. She entered the Mystery, becoming an angel of her own. Some looked up, sensing Mira's energy above them. They longed to see some glimpse of her as she departed. With their human eyes unable to see her energy without form, they scanned for some other confirmation of her passage. Some sensed the transition in their own energy field; others understood. Indescribable bliss swaddled Mira's spirit.

As she ascended through the blinding-white light surrounding and lifting her, Mira's awareness came upon a lifeless form lying still below her. A young man, a boy really, mortally wounded and alone, lay motionless in the soft grass next to a field of war. He wore the uniform of another nation's army, and his instruments of war lay useless around him. His body had grown cold, the soil beneath him drenched in his own lifeblood. His broken spirit remained trapped in a limbo of nothingness as if frozen in time. Overriding shame invaded his barren form, infused into his shattered spirit, with his essence bound up in a fatal shroud of self-loathing.

Mira knew this soul. She'd traveled the millennia with this soul. She and this soul were one. Destiny, Beshert, moved Mira to release this entrapped spirit into the same light she now occupied, just as he helped guide her in her journey before. To do so, she had to channel the messages he'd brought to her in the bleak moments of her overdose.

Mira reached down to touch the spirit of Jakob and intoned:

Lieber, you misunderstood:
You had a higher mission.
Lieber, it is your destiny.
Remember why you came.
You came to carry the word of the Mystery beyond all Mysteries.
You came knowing you were not to destroy life during your time here.
You came this time to protect life.
You came this time to raise others up.
You came this time to raise yourself up.
You came this time to act in love.
You came this time to be love.
You came to teach peace.
You came to teach peace.
You came to teach peace.

Mira sent the universe's healing energy into the trapped spirit of the young Hessian soldier. Then, Jakob gently separated and lifted from the empty form below him. He joined Mira and moved with her into the blazing light. And as they moved higher into the light, it grew even more brilliant and vibrated with loving energy. Finally, their two energies weaved together into a single, brilliant ruby red braid and dissolved into the Mystery beyond all Mysteries.